THE SUBSTITUTE BRIDE

I0521334

Maggie Award Finalist

Mackinac Island Romances Series –
Associated Novella

THE SUBSTITUTE BRIDE

Mackinac Island Romances Series –
Associated Novella

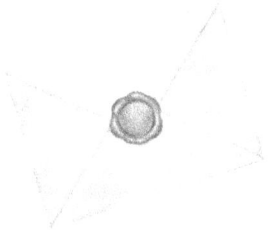

By **Carrie Fancett Pagels**

HEARTS OVERCOMING PRESS

First Edition
October 2015
ISBN-13: 978-0-997190830
ISBN-10: 0997190833

Hearts Overcoming Press

Cover Art by Hearts Overcoming Press, 2023

Published in the United States of America

Dedication

To Teresa Mathews, an amazing lady—a beautiful woman inside and out.
I thank God for your sweet spirit and friendship!

&

In Memory of Carlton Mathews, a godly man who blessed so many.
Gone too soon.

Characters

This novella has a full cast of characters. Note: Poor House/County Farm refers to the same location.

Louis (Smith) Penwell – hero, railroad manager
    Abner Smith (Penwell) – hero's deceased father

    Andrew Ellison – railroad investor and executive
    Cora – Louis's pen pal and Sonja's friend, deceased

Sonja Hoeke – heroine, substitute mail carrier for her father
    Mr. Hoeke – Sonja's father, recently injured while delivering mail to the Poor House

    Mr. McLaughlin – postmaster
    Mr. Akers – elderly gentleman and husband of Sonja's childhood Sunday school teacher

    Sonja's friends – Christina Spivey, Mamie Pettit, Lila Swanson, Letitia Brown

Poor House director – Iris Geisig
    Poor Farm residents – Ronald, Joanna and Liisa

Mrs. Peter Welling, the late Mr. Welling's daughter-in-law, Mackinac Island resident
    Mr. Welling, recently deceased, farmer and neighbor to the County Farm

Deborah Mitchell – Inn owner's daughter

Mysterious woman – I'm not telling! (See Author's Notes in the back!)

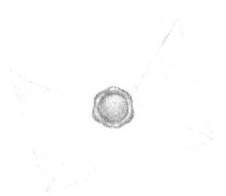

Chapter One

Shepherd, Michigan
November 1891

Sonja closed the post office's heavy oak door behind her, shutting out the frigid breeze that had accompanied her. The blessed heat from the pot-bellied stove, center left, drew her closer. She trod across the wide-planked pine floors and then extended her hands toward the warmth.

Bent behind the high, dark-stained counter, Mr. McLaughlin, the postmaster, glanced up over his spectacles. "Glad to see ye, lass."

With no decorations, other than a few posters tacked to the wood-paneled walls, the Spartan room lay empty. From the fresh beeswax scent, the postal superintendent had already waxed the few furnishings in the room—a narrow table for folks to set boxes on, a straight-backed oak chair where elderly patrons could sit, and the counter.

"Has it been quiet this morning, Mr. McLaughlin?" Her words almost echoed in the chamber.

"Give it a few weeks, lass, as folks realize they need to get their Christmas parcels out."

"That's what Father says, too." Among other things he often discussed, such as her need to find employment and to not merely be his substitute at the post office. "Hard to believe there's already snow dusting the streets, sir."

"Could be a hard winter." He shuffled through a few envelopes. "Folks in these parts got their maple syrup to market just fine—and that'll make the difference between hungry bellies and full ones this winter. Aye?"

"Yes, I pray so." Sonja strode away from the stove and toward the postmaster, shivering.

Conversation about Shepherd's maple syrup always reminded her of the tragedy a decade earlier. An entire boatload of men had gone down in the river, their precious syrup lost, and one man, Abner Smith, dead. Where was his son, Louis, now? How did someone come to grips with losing everything—as Louis had? Sonja nibbled her lower lip. She was about to find out for herself what it was like to lose everything—if Father carried out his threats.

"How's yer Pa faring today?" Mr. McLaughlin smoothed his bushy white moustache.

Ornery, demanding she find a husband, threatening to kick her out—just like her friend Cora had said he would do. But Cora was gone now. Buried in a pauper's grave. Sonja blinked back tears.

"Ah, now, lass—he'll be fine soon."

Obviously, he misunderstood her grief over her friend as fear for her father.

She dipped her chin.

Mr. McLaughlin tugged at his stiff, celluloid collar. "I need to head out back for a moment." He jerked a stubby thumb over his narrow shoulder.

"Yes, sir."

The silver-haired man pushed aside the curtains that separated the front office from the rear workroom. "I'll return shortly, lass."

Sonja circled behind the desk and reached for the stack of unfiled letters. Her heart leapt in her chest as she spied the top one—with Cora's name. Sonja slid the missive closer.

Mr. Penwell's distinctive and elegant handwriting marked him as the sender. The poor man—his pen pal had died, but he didn't yet know in far off South Dakota where he lived.

Would she, or possibly even her father, get into trouble if she opened the letter? This was, after all her father's livelihood and she represented him when she substituted on his route. Sonja's mouth went dry.

She exhaled a low sigh as sweet Mr. Akers opened the heavy door and entered the building, a heavy beaver coat draped over one arm, his cane looped over the other.

"Good day, Little Sunshine." He greeted her with the same nickname he'd given Sonja when she was a child in his wife's Sunday school class, more than twenty years earlier. A class Sonja now taught. Hard to believe Mrs. Akers had been gone to heaven for four years already.

"How are you, sir?" She watched as he laid the glossy coat on the counter.

"Perplexed, my dear, and disturbed." He removed his tall, black hat and set it beside the coat.

"Oh dear, why are you mystified, Mr. Akers?" *And why had he brought the fur here?*

He leaned in and stroked his white beard. "Your father."

She cringed, anticipating what the elderly man might say. *Father wouldn't. He didn't. He probably had.* "Please tell me he hasn't asked you to marry me, sir."

His aquamarine eyes widened. "How did you know, Sunshine?"

Groaning, she shook her head slowly.

"Well, of course that wouldn't work, my Sunny Girl, since I think of you like a daughter—or maybe even a granddaughter. And because of that, I am about fed up with your father's efforts to marry you off." He leaned on his silver, wolf's-headed cane, shaking his head. "And now this latest ridiculous effort of your father's, which I'm sure Mr. McLaughlin has shared with you."

"I haven't heard, sir." *Now what?* She braced herself.

"Glad I came in, and happy McLaughlin's not here right now." Mr. Akers narrowed his eyes. "Your father is seeking employment for you at the new post office way over in Pinetown—or anyplace further north—and is saying he'll put you out of his home if you're not married by Christmas."

"What?" Humiliation heated her cheeks.

"If I weren't a widower, I'd offer you a place at my house and look after you." His silver brows rose high. "But you know people would talk, Sonja."

"Yes, sir, I do." She tapped her fingernails on the countertop. *What on earth is happening with Father?*

Mr. Akers patted the long coat. "People can gossip all they want about you wearing this fur. But it will keep you warm on your route, my dear, and we don't want you coming down ill like Cora, poor soul."

Sonja closed her eyes for a moment. "I miss her." *Ached for her companionship.* She missed Cora so much more than she'd missed even her closest sister, all of whom were married and gone. And all of whom delighted in tormenting her as they grew up in their domineering father's household.

"Cora was a good friend to you." Mr. Akers sighed and held the fur aloft. "The coat may be too short for you, since you're so tall, and my wife was a normal-sized woman."

Which meant Sonja was abnormal, as she knew. At almost six feet tall, she'd had a number of men imply that she was somehow defective, although Mr. Akers didn't speak his words in an unkind way.

"Thank you, sir." Father had ceased buying her new clothing a few years earlier, once she'd reached twenty-five, stating that she could easily find a husband to provide for her if she'd only be amenable.

"I'll be praying for you, Sunshine." He placed his hat back on his head, walked toward the door, and left, allowing a brief chill wind to enter.

Pulsing with anger at her father, Sonja's hands shook as she grabbed a letter opener and did the unthinkable—slit open a piece of mail addressed to someone else—to her friend, Cora. She scanned Mr. Penwell's words, written to a woman he hadn't realized was dying.

My dear friend, Cora,

It should come as no surprise that I would like to extend an offer of marriage to you. Your recent letters lead me to believe you are considering this possibility, too. I fear I am in a situation that now requires me to take a bride very quickly for a new, and elevated, position I am being considered for. My supervisor indicates a stable, married man must be placed in this prime railroad position. Would you write back to me immediately with your reply, so I might anticipate your arrival?

She scanned the next few lines, which referenced some of Cora's recent letters written to him. Cora hadn't lied to Mr. Penwell, but certainly she'd stretched the truth or had implied more than was true. *Oh dear.* Teaching Sunday school? Dancing? Yes, Sonja had insisted her friend come out with her to a barn dance—during which both of them watched from the sidelines. And Cora had once sat in on Sonja's Sunday school class. But the letter made it sound like more, somehow.

Inside, was a bank draft. Sonja sucked in a breath at the large sum written on it. She looked around the room, expecting someone to appear to snatch it from her and accuse her of stealing. Then, she shoved the letter hastily into the deep pocket of her skirt.

What would it be like if she were to take Cora's place and become Mr. Penwell's bride? Dare she make the suggestion? Or should she suffer the embarrassment of being put out of the only home she'd ever known and shipped off to another town?

Of course, she wouldn't cash his check but use her own funds to travel west. Before she lost her nerve, Sonja opened her private drawer and retrieved her writing implements and stationary. She hastily penned a missive back to Mr. Penwell. Once the ink dried she folded it, put the letter in an envelope, sealed it, and purchased a stamp, placing her money in the cash drawer. On impulse, she went ahead and affixed the postmark, then set the letter into the outgoing mail container.

Heart pounding, Sonja drew in the room's clean scent and imagined herself traveling by train almost all the way across the country. A log in the stove shifted and rumbled. What would it be like to leave central Michigan, where she'd grown up? Would Mr. Penwell even consider a substitute bride?

Mr. McLaughlin returned, his heavy soles pounding a steady beat across the floor as he pulled a wheeled cart filled with mail. "Thanks for holding down the fort for me, Miss Hoeke."

"You're welcome, sir." A fortress away from her father was just what she needed.

The postmaster rolled the cart near the wall then grabbed her father's bag. "Here's yer Pa's duffle. Not too heavy, or I'd carry it out for you."

She accepted it and then stuffed the sack with the missives from the counter.

Her supervisor's gaze fell on her "new" coat and he frowned. "Looks familiar."

"Mr. Akers is so sweet. He brought me his wife's coat to use for the rural route."

The postmaster exhaled loudly. "No doubt your father asked Walter to propose, too."

She bit her lip.

"Never fear, we're working out a position for you as a full time postal assistant above the straits."

"What?" The question came out harsher than she wanted. "I mean, where in the Upper Peninsula, Mr. McLaughlin?

"Actually, between the straits, on Mackinac Island—at least for the summer."

"Mackinac Island?" That was where the Wellings' son, Peter, and his wife, owned a large inn. According to old Mr. Welling, God rest his soul, his daughter-in-law descended from the wealthy Cadottes and had many family members who populated the island.

"Yes, your pa said you wanted to give him and your ma some solitude and asked if I'd recommend you. Which, of course, I'd be happy to do."

So, she'd be shipped up north. At least she wasn't going to be assigned to the Upper Peninsula. Above the Straits it was much colder and snowier than Shepherd, in central Michigan, in wintertime. And she would know one family on the island. But would young Mrs. Welling be busy with her own extended Cadotte family? Sonja blinked back tears. She'd hoped that Father's notion of having the house to himself would pass, but it hadn't. And Sonja prayed that her father would retire and let her continue to carry the route— if Mr. McLaughlin agreed.

"I can see by your face that you didn't ask for that position at all, lass." He sighed deeply.

"No."

"Thought you were one of those gals who wanted her own route and not as a backup."

"No, sir."

"I thought that's why you have always been so diligent in substituting."

She stiffened at his use of the word *substituting*. Did he know she'd signed her letter, "A Possible Substitute"? She'd need a position in South Dakota, so she could get to know Mr. Penwell better, before they married—if he chose to take her up on his offer. But first she needed to make sure she received any mail sent to her friend. "I need a favor, Mr. McLaughlin. And it involves the mail."

He cocked his head. "What is it, lass?"

"Might I accept any further correspondence for Cora? She has...had...no next of kin, and I was her closest friend."

The postmaster's quizzical expression softened. "I dinna see why not. Ye can be sure and certain that Iris won't notify what few friends the poor woman had. Nay trouble—I'll keep 'em right here for you." He slid open a narrow drawer where he stored an extra watch, scissors, and an ambrotype image of his Scottish mother.

"Thank you, sir." Sonja drew in a deep breath. *God, you know I need help. Please show me I did the right thing.*

Chapter Two

*T*he queasiness in Louis's gut had nothing to do with this train but everything to do with it rocking along toward their final destination—his nightmare. He drew in a deep, steadying breath, and touched the small Bible in the pocket of his best wool suit.

"Ever ride in the luxury car before, Mr. Penwell?" Andrew Ellison's deep voice held conflicting notes of sympathy and humor.

Louis sat up straighter in his heavily cushioned, plush seat. "No, sir."

The railway investor sucked in deeply on his cigar and then exhaled slowly. "Well, get used to it. With this promotion you'll always be able to choose the executive compartment from here on out."

"It's certainly well-appointed, Mr. Ellison." On the far wall, a built-in buffed-to-a-gleam cherry wood cabinet housed a full array of crystal and silver pieces. Crystal brandy snifters and liquor bottles sparkled as they rocked slightly in the high-sided, mahogany tray atop the counter.

"Should be for the money we put into this." The investor narrowed his eyes and leaned forward, spreading his legs apart. "But you don't seem to be enjoying the trip."

Louis raised a palm. "Oh, no, sir, I am grateful for the promotion."

"Your face says otherwise."

"How could I not appreciate the luxury of this room—crystal carafes and our own refreshment bar, comfortable sleeping quarters and seats?"

"Perhaps it's just the motion of the train giving you that sallow look." Mr. Ellison's pipe smoke drifted in Louis's direction, bringing to mind the scent of his father's favorite tobacco, a rich Virginia blend harvested in the area where the prominent Penwell family's plantations had dominated for centuries.

"I'm not accustomed to traveling much by rail, despite my job." Louis grabbed onto the excuse.

"You're no longer stuck in South Dakota, with so few women as possible brides. And with that raise you should be a married man in no time at all and a good influence in the community—as your supervisor figures."

Or not. His mouth grew dry. He'd not heard back from Cora about his proposal, and now he was on his way there. What if she cashed the check and was even now headed out to South Dakota? Everything had happened so quickly, he'd not had time to do much other than pack his belongings. Cora was not an impulsive woman, from what he could discern in the letters. At least he'd gotten a telegram sent.

Ellison rose and crossed the chamber to the wall cabinet and poured himself a tumbler of whiskey. "You've been away from your hometown too long, I hear."

Louis's gut clenched. Hometown? He had no hometown. "The home where I lived in Salt River burned, sir." Not that it mattered, since he'd lost their temporary home when his father had drowned in the river. They'd moved to Salt River after his mother died and Father had finally ceased gambling and taken a job at the mill. But then his father died, too. And just recently, Louis's benefactor in

Michigan, Mr. Welling, also passed away. Except for his friend, Cora, Louis truly was alone in the world.

Ellison sipped his drink, which sloshed in the snifter with the train's steady movement. "I'm a Michigander myself, and Shepherd has become a bustling railroad center."

"Haven't been back since I left." Louis's gut began to roil, and the train's movement shuddered through him.

"No?" The man quirked an eyebrow. "Mr. Stewart was sure you'd jump at the chance to return home."

Louis stifled the urge to cringe. "Is that why my supervisor recommended me for the job in Michigan?"

"Precisely."

Mr. Stewart had always seemed so fond of Louis. "I have to admit, it came as a surprise." Louis would rather have remained where he was and had Cora join him. He prayed Cora had received his telegram.

If only his supervisor had realized that he was sending him back to the one place he'd vowed never to visit again, to never set foot in again, much less in which to reside. When Louis had learned Cora corresponded from the Poor House outside Shepherd, he'd vowed that one day he'd rescue her from the place. *Why God?* Perhaps this disruption was for Cora. But would the townsfolk accept her as a prominent railroad man's wife or still see her as the woman from the Poor Farm? Would they recognize him and view him as the boy from the Poor House, with no family to claim him? A boy called Louis Smith because his father wouldn't use his Penwell name.

"We had another board member, not someone I personally know, who requested your services in Shepherd." Ellison arched a brow at him. "We need a new man there. One with your excellent head for business."

"Thank you. I've tried to work hard." Work was all he did. If work was like a sickness, it had been with Louis. In his Bible reading the night before, Solomon's words in

Ecclesiastes had convicted him, "Better is an handful with quietness, than both the hands full with travail and vexation of spirit," which certainly applied to his case.

"Would you like a drink? Please, help yourself, Louis."

Other men drank. Some smoked opium, even. Some ran after women. Louis worked long hours and when he wasn't working, he was at church—working there. "I'll just have some seltzer water, thank you." He patted his stomach.

"Ah, yes, a good idea." Ellison settled back into his chair and opened up the newspaper he'd brought on board.

Rising, Louis straightened his pants legs. After he adjusted to the train's movement, he retrieved a tumbler of seltzer water and then returned to his seat.

Rest in me. Louis glanced at his companion in the cabin, but the man's thin lips hadn't moved. *Rest. In. Me.* Goose bumps rose up on his arms, beneath his shirt and heavy jacket.

Mr. Ellison lowered his paper, folded it and placed it on his lap. Soon his eyelids began to lower, his head nodded, and then he began to snore.

Louis retrieved and opened his packet of letters from Cora, trying to imagine how their meeting might go. Although they'd corresponded for some time, only recently had she mentioned something about performing occasional work as a substitute mail carrier. That hadn't made sense, since the Poor Farm normally required the inmates to work. But Cora's handwriting had become so shaky that perhaps Louis had misread her words. The matron of the Poor House had certainly tried to squeeze every last ounce of labor out of him the year he'd been imprisoned there. He'd not been in jail—but it felt like he'd been.

Cora's recent assertion that she'd been regularly attending the Christian Church, occasionally assisting in teaching Sunday school classes, also seemed out of character for someone who had been struggling with her faith. Perhaps their correspondence, in which he'd discussed the Bible, had found some fertile ground. The oddest thing Cora had mentioned was that she was dancing again—or had at least attended a dance. Yet, she'd said she was lame and likely would always be so. But God was a God of miracles, so who was he to question? Hadn't he questioned this move with the railroad? He'd been in a cold sweat since he'd learned of his destination.

He was looking forward to finally meeting his writing friend in person. All of these concerns could be put to rest before they married. Then, maybe someday soon, they could find a position elsewhere, away from the Hades of his youth.

Chapter Three

*T*he sun hid behind clouds that threatened snow, on Sonja's third day in a row of substituting for her father. In his mid-sixties, and in frequent poor health, Father should retire and let her carry the route. Instead, he wanted her gone. She nibbled her lower lip. *I will not cry. I will not.* Admitting to herself that her father didn't care for her had freed Sonja to begin looking for ways out. Cora had encouraged her to look beyond her current situation. Directing her mare down the street to the post office, Sonja spied several of her Ladies' Aid friends outside May's Confectionary Shoppe. Boxes of chocolates, fudge, and taffy crowded the window display where the young women clustered. Were they hoping a beau would send them a treat this Christmas? Would Mr. Penwell be generous? Would he buy her candy for special occasions? Or even just to say he cared? But how could he care—he didn't even know her.

Christina Spivey yelled, "Don't forget the Christmas pageant committee at Mamie Pettit's house."

Beside her, pretty, red-haired Lila cupped her hands around her mouth to amplify her breathy voice, "This Saturday afternoon."

"I'll be there," Sonja called out, as she directed the mare on. How she'd miss her friends when she was gone. But with them all married, she saw them less and less. She, Christina, and Lila were the only young women in the group of mostly elderly ladies.

When the light carriage rounded the corner, one of the laborers her father had tried to connect her with eyed her. Even at this early hour, he tipped back a pocket bottle of what he called his "medicine" but which she knew contained whiskey. Would Mr. Penwell share this same bad habit? Sonja gritted her teeth. She'd made a rash decision. And were there wild Indians in South Dakota? She didn't know. The poor tribe members in her state were being treated like criminals, forced onto reservations and their children sent off to schools—away from their families. She shook the sudden stiffness in her shoulders.

Directing the mare to pull the buggy alongside the post office building, Sonja blinked as snowflakes lit upon her brow. This would be a chilly ride. If only she had her dog with her. Darren used to accompany her and nestle on the floorboard at her feet. But her sister had taken Sonja's pet, with no protest from either of her parents. Moisture threatened to turn to tears in her eyes, and Sonja forced herself to offer a smile as the postmaster exited the post office and carried her father's bag to her.

"There ye go, lass." Mr. McLaughlin arranged the canvas bag so that it lay flat on the carriage bed.

"Father doesn't want me riding his horse." Although it might be easier for deliveries.

The postmaster raised one shaggy eyebrow. "Of course not, lass. This little cart is what ye'll need, and it's sturdy enough even for the County Farm drive."

She cringed, remembering how rutted the road was. "Yes, but will my teeth be jarred out of my mouth?"

The silver-haired Scotsman sighed deeply. "Iris sees no need to waste money on leveling the road, as she rarely has visitors. But I'll give her another warning."

"Father was beside himself when he was thrown last week because of that deep hole in the road."

15

"The magistrate dinna think too kindly of it, either." The postmaster sighed heavily. "Thank the good Lord ye are such a sturdy lass and can help yer pa."

Sturdy. Not exactly a complimentary word, although the postal superintendent surely meant it to be. Sonja towered over all the women in town and many of the men. "Yes, sir."

"Tell Iris if she willna fix it, then she'll have to send someone out to the road to collect her mail from a box, and she'll nay like that, I assure you." Mr. McLaughlin pulled his watch from the front pocket of his navy blue jacket and flipped the cover open. "Ye best be on yer way—the skies shout snow, lass."

She extended her gloved palm, where one snowflake drifted onto it. "Those snowflakes are coming!" Sonja flicked the reins on the gray mare's back and off they went, the bag at her feet jostling about, even on the town road, which was fairly level.

As she passed the telegram office, a square, log building, the operator came out. "Miss Hoeke, can you stop?"

Had Mr. Penwell already responded to her letter? No, it would take much longer for the letter to have reached him.

As she brought her horse to a stop, Mr. Hood strode to the side of the buggy. The distinguished-looking man waved a telegram in front of her. "Could you take a look at this? It was for your friend, Cora, and came in while I was out sick."

So many had been ill with sickness and some had died. Mr. Hood's wife was fortunate she'd not lost her husband. "A telegram?"

"My assistant decided to put it aside. But I'm wondering if we oughtn't notify this man, Mr. Penwell, that Cora is gone."

Sonja accepted the telegram and scanned its contents. *Stay put. Am on way to Shepherd. Louis*

Her heart began to pound in her chest. The poor man was on his way here to collect his bride, but Cora was gone.

He must want desperately to marry her. Tears pricked her eyes. Poor Cora. Poor man. And here Sonja had thought Mr. Penwell might accept her as a substitute. Who had she been fooling? She chewed her lower lip. And Cora buried in a pauper's grave—if only Sonja had saved enough money to have her interred elsewhere. How awful that would be to take Cora's friend there, but Sonja would.

"I'll have to meet him when he arrives." She swallowed. "And I'll do my duty and take him to her grave, have no fear."

Mr. Hood shook his head. "Cora might not even get to stay put, Sonja."

A chill shot up her spine. "What do you mean?"

His strong facial features tugged, but he said nothing.

"Why would Cora's body be moved?"

"She's in a pauper's grave, Sonja." Mr. Hood's low, serious tone raised the hair on the back of her neck. "That means those body grabbers from the university will want to dig her up for their medical studies."

"No!" she gasped. It was insult enough that Cora had no proper headstone. "Do you really think they shall?"

"Last night we got a request through the county board committee." His high cheekbones flushed red.

She'd paid for her friend's medical treatment but hadn't been able to afford a plot. With her earnings, Sonja had saved enough for a very small headstone—but what could she do if the state grave diggers came? *Lord help me.* God's word said He knew their every need. She'd have to trust Him with this, too. Sonja forced back tears.

"I guess I was hoping to ask this fella, Penwell, when he gets to town, if he might be willing to pay for a proper plot. I'm hoping he's kin. Is he?" As the sun peeked through the snow clouds, Mr. Hood squinted at her.

"No. I'm afraid not." If things went as she'd hoped, he'd have been her future husband. It all seemed absurd now.

"Well, you keep that message—you were her closest friend. And after she got so ill, she'd told me to give any telegrams to you if they came through."

"Thank you, Mr. Hood. Have a good day." She clucked her tongue and slapped the reins against the mare's back.

Apprehension niggled at Sonja as the mare pulled the carriage onto the county road that led to the Poor Farm and then to her last stop, the Wellings' large farm. This would be her first contact with Mrs. Geisig since Cora's funeral. Cora, an inmate at the farm, had been sick for months. There would be no more outgoing letters from her to her pen pal, Mr. Penwell, her only communicant in the outside world. Sonja had been at Cora's side when she passed from earth to heaven. Her last words had been about Louis Penwell— "Tell him I'm sorry."

Something in her spirit troubled Sonja. She directed the horse to pull the cart to the side of the road and reached for the last two packets to be delivered. One to the Welling farm and one slim batch to Mrs. Geisig. Sonja untied the twine that held five slim missives together. A letter for little Liisa, a card for Joanna, and a college notification for Ronald— wouldn't that be wonderful if he was accepted? Then, at the bottom, a slim letter for Cora.

Sonja ran her finger over her friend's name. Gone. And only forty two years old. Although there had been fifteen years between them, Cora's youthful spirit and vivacity, despite her illness, had always drawn Sonja to her. They could talk about anything and everything, although Cora initially would have nothing to do with hearing God's word. A tear escaped and Sonja wiped it away. Cora and the Lord had settled their differences before she'd gone home to Glory, and for that she'd be forever grateful. Sonja sniffed. She'd take this letter home, too, as she had the other. She was still violating the postal rules. But she had peace that God wouldn't mind. And Mr. MacLaughlin had already told her it would be fine.

The mare snorted as Sonja removed her soft gloves and then opened the letter.

Dear Cora,

I hope you don't believe me impatient. I pray you received my other letter and I await your reply. Today I was informed of the position I shall assume, and it is a remarkable one. I leave you with this scripture, my friend, for I find that my supervisor is correct, such a job requires what Solomon so eloquently wrote: There is one alone, and there is not a second; yea, he hath neither child nor brother: yet is there no end of all his labour; neither is his eye satisfied with riches; neither saith he, For whom do I labour, and bereave my soul of good? This is also vanity, yea, it is a sore travail.

Two are better than one; because they have a good reward for their labour. For if they fall, the one will lift up his fellow: but woe to him that is alone when he falleth; for he hath not another to help him up.

Not very romantic.

Sonja slipped the letter into her reticule, then tucked it beneath her skirts, and urged her horse on. While there was indeed truth in those Bible verses, was this Mr. Penwell a stodgy older man whose idea of a lovely evening was sitting in front of the fire and quoting her the Bible? She imagined an Ebenezer Scrooge type of individual with long strands of silver hair plastered to his head, bent over his pile of gold, all the while stealing glances at his Bible. She shivered.

Maybe he'd never receive her missive. Maybe all would work out well on Mackinac Island. Maybe God had another plan. She flicked the reins and moved on.

Enduring the bone-rattling drive to the Poor Farm, she drove past fields already harvested by the few inhabitants of the home. Hay had already been harvested from both their farm and the Wellings' property months earlier. Mr. Welling always did this chore for Iris Geisig, never charging her a fee, which the plump woman usually crowed over. Ahead, the huge white Victorian farmhouse loomed, looking for all the world like the happy home of wealthy farmers. *Appearances certainly could be deceiving.* Sonja's heart clenched as she approached, wagon wheels groaning over the uneven road. Liisa and Joanna paused in stacking wood, at the side of the house, and waved at her. Cora was gone, buried in the Potter's Field. And her body possibly about to be used in some university studies. Sonja shivered all the way down to her high boot tops.

The proprietress wriggled out the front door, her enormous bustle requiring a tug. "Finally here, eh?"

Resisting the temptation to tell the woman to have her drive repaired and then the mail would arrive earlier, Sonja pulled out the re-tied bundle of correspondence.

Iris snatched the letters. "I've got a box of Cora's things for you. Let me get it." The coarse woman disappeared into the house, slamming the door behind her.

She'd not had the chance to tell Mrs. Geisig about Mr. McLaughlin's warning that she must repair her drive. Sonja shook her head and rocked on the porch in her black, lace-up boots, hoping to warm her toes. Curlicues and all manner of elaborate gingerbread details gave the house a deceptively charming appearance. Even when Cora was constantly coughing, she'd been forced to paint the railing out here. Sonja had assisted her on one of her substitute mail carrier missions, returning to the Poor House after she'd delivered the Wellings' mail, which was the last stop on the route.

A tall, blond young man strode up from the barn. She waved to Ronald.

"Will you come back to tutor me tonight?" The seventeen-year-old wiped sweat from his brow with the back of his arm.

"Sorry. Not tonight. But after church?"

He frowned. "Iris says we can't go this week because we've gone three times in a row…"

"Which costs her good feed money," she completed the statement for him, having heard the absurd explanation before.

Mr. Welling, the neighboring farmer, used to supply Mrs. Geisig with additional feed and hay for her horses after she'd complained about the animals needing extra feed for the church trips. But, even before the generous man had died, the matron had given different excuses as to why the inhabitants couldn't attend services.

"I'll drive out one day next week, then, after chores are done."

He grinned, but then his angular features formed a serious expression. "Did you see anything from the Michigan Normal School?"

Sonja rolled her lips together.

"I know you're not supposed to look, but…"

She grinned the unspoken response. One letter had been addressed to him from the school.

He beamed. "Thanks, Miss Hoeke, you're a peach."

Ronald ran off behind the house. Sonja stepped from the porch, and looked up at the third floor center window. Cora's room. At least Iris had allowed Sonja to pay for extra help and for Cora's doctor. Mrs. Geisig hadn't forced her friend to go into town for her final days, which showed some good will on her part—either that or she wanted the money from the county for Cora's room and board.

The Poor Farm matron returned and shoved a small wooden crate at her. "Take it."

Startled, Sonja pulled up to her full height. "Thank you."

"No need to thank me." The woman's beady eyes glossed over with moisture. Had she actually possessed some compassion for Cora? "Too bad she'll not be here for that Christmas pageant you're always pushing on us."

When the woman sniffed, Sonja lowered her head. "We need the girls and Ronald to come in Sunday for church so I can measure them for their costumes. And I'll be glad to pick them up and bring them back home that day." Perhaps that would assuage the woman's concerns and get the youth into town.

"That'd be fine." She swiveled toward the door, shoving her bustle down as she wedged through the doorframe. "Got supper to cook."

Again, the door was slammed shut behind the woman. Sonja held the lightweight box—all that was left of Cora's earthly treasures. How could this be the sum total of someone's existence?

She strode through the yard, got back into the carriage, and directed the mare onto the bumpy drive. Then they turned back onto the county road and delivered mail to the Wellings' home, the last on her route. Old Mr. Welling's daughter-in-law, from Mackinac Island, was there clearing out the house and preparing it for winter now that Mr. Welling had passed on.

The scent of freshly baked bread, and something scintillatingly chocolate, wafted through the screened door on the porch as Sonja carried their mail up.

Sweet-faced young Mrs. Welling opened the door. "Why, Sonja, it's so good to see you, but I take it this means your father has been hurt badly."

"I'm afraid enough so that he's off his feet for now. Dr. Queen says he may not be able to return to work for another week." The baked goods inside tempted her senses and made her stomach grumble. Mother had recently stopped baking any desserts at home, concerned that Sonja's father may have diabetes.

Mrs. Welling laughed. "Come in and have some cookies and milk. I'm baking them for the church before I leave town. Chocolate crinkles. My father-in-law would have wanted to contribute to the upcoming celebrations."

Sonja grinned. This woman, who'd visited annually since she'd married Peter Welling, always made Sonja feel like she was a girl again—and a welcome visitor rather than a spinster who substituted for her father's mail route.

She followed the beautiful dark-haired lady inside. When Sonja bent to sit at the table, the telegram to Cora slipped out of her pocket. Mrs. Welling bent to retrieve it before Sonja could. As she held it out to her, the woman's gaze seemed to settle on the addressee.

Sonja accepted the telegram back. "Cora was my closest friend. Mr. Hood gave me the message." My, she sounded defensive even to herself.

Mrs. Welling slid into the Queen Anne chair across from Sonja. "Is that from Louis, the young man from the Poor House that my father-in-law helped? Had Cora known him from before?"

"No, this is Mr. Penwell—Louis Penwell—and they'd never met." The overpowering scent of the fresh baked cookies made Sonja's mouth water. "Cora got his name and address from a railroad magazine and took up correspondence with him. Her husband had worked with trains before he died."

The pretty woman's dark eyes widened. "A railroad worker, you say?"

"Yes, Mr. Penwell and Cora had been corresponding for quite some time." Viewing the confusion on Mrs. Welling's face, she asked, "Do you know him?"

The young woman shook her head. "I know my father-in-law and someone else assisted a young man named Louis through college, after his father died."

An hour later, when Sonja left, confusion and loss of focus over Mrs. Welling's comments about Louis still plagued her. That night, and the next day, she mulled over Mrs. Welling's suspicions. And although she couldn't do anything about where Cora was interred, she picked up the headstone for her grave, intent upon having Mr. Penwell accompany her when she placed it. According to the railroad office, he should arrive tomorrow.

Then she'd know who he *really* was.

Chapter Four

*L*ouis disembarked the train. As the smoke cleared, he spied a blonde woman almost as tall as himself, pacing, a bundle clutched in her arm. Could it be? Sonja Hoeke? He'd always had a soft spot for the gangly girl who tagged after her older sisters only to be treated like an unwanted cat. But this woman was dressed in an old-fashioned, beaver coat. Sonja had been such a pretty girl, with large green eyes and thick blonde hair. But she'd not remember him. He'd been the boy at the Poor Farm, an orphan.

The young woman drew closer. His heart leapt to his throat. He'd been wrong—stunning was a better description for this Grecian goddess. Statuesque and beautiful. Sonja wasn't simply pretty; she *dazzled* as sun glinted off her golden hair.

But Louis had made his offer of marriage to Cora. He shouldn't even be considering the fact that now, as a railroad executive, he might finally have a chance with Sonja. But he couldn't help the thought. Cora had mentioned that Sonja was her friend. Had she referred to her as Miss Hoeke? Was she yet single? Impossible. It didn't matter—he'd proposed to another. And knowing the irascible Mr. Hoeke, he likely kept her at home to serve whatever needs he had. In public, Mr. Hoeke had taken to treating her like a cross between an

25

unloved son and a servant, having her fetch whatever he needed but never offering her a kind word.

She strode toward him, the fur coat hitting her at an unfashionable mid-calf length. Probably one of her sister's cast-offs, although it could even be her mother's or grandmother's.

Sonja waited, an expectant look on her face.

"Are you Mr. Penwell?" She blinked rapidly and chewed on her lower lip. "Louis Penwell?"

"Yes, I am. Were you a friend of Cora's?" He knew she was, but his tongue didn't seem to be working properly.

"Yes. I'm Sonja—Cora's friend." She scanned his face. Did she recognize him? They'd attended school together only briefly, but they'd been members at church together during the time he'd lived in Salt River. She averted her gaze to the railway platform. "Why don't you get your luggage and then we'll talk."

Sonja sat on the depot bench, awaiting Mr. Penwell's return.

Much younger and more handsome than she'd imagined, Louis topped her height by a few inches. His dark curly hair begged to be tucked up under his hat and his chocolate brown eyes meshed nicely with his ruddy complexion. She'd expected someone closer to Cora's age and with streaks of gray in his hair—or Ebenezer Scrooge personified. She held back a laugh.

So he'd not received her letter and now he was here, in Shepherd—looking for Cora. The previous evening, she'd read Louis's letters to Cora, looking for hints to their relationship. All were rather banal, simply correspondents discussing railway work and life in general. One missive had taken her aback—when Louis asked why Cora had recommended Sonja to him as another pen pal.

Perhaps Cora had been looking out for her friends' interests—both Sonja's and Louis's—for when she'd gone on to her heavenly rewards.

Sonja clutched the petite, but heavy, mortuary stone to her chest. When he'd seen it, her father had belittled it by asking, "Who would visit that woman's grave besides you?"

Here was Louis Penwell. Surely he would go to the grave with her to pay his respects.

The broad-shouldered man returned, easily carrying what appeared to be a heavy trunk. Mr. Penwell strode with self-assurance, but fleeting irritation skittered over his features. "I'm sorry, but I'm going to need to tag this and have it delivered to my office right away. Somehow I'd forgotten I'd need my books and other things to conduct my work." He rubbed his chin. "Can you wait a few moments more?"

She nodded her assent, her hat ribbons blown into her face by a chill wind. Despite the sooty air at the train station, she could swear that the scent of snow lingered. Sonja settled on a wooden bench. What should she say?

When Louis returned, Sonja pointed to the seat beside her. "I think you'd best sit down, Mr. Penwell."

"Please, call me Louis." He searched her face. A crease formed between his dark eyebrows.

Something in his eyes forced her recollection of the one boy at school and at church who she didn't tower over. Could it be—was Mrs. Welling's assertion correct that this man was Louis Smith? "Oh?"

"We do share history."

She sucked in a breath, waiting—could it be? Was this fine-looking man the kind youth she'd known as Louis Smith?

"We are both stalwart friends of Cora."

Were friends. Exhaling, tears began to trickle down her face. How could she tell him? "Cora was a dear friend of mine. Of both of ours."

"Was?" His voice emerged in a rasp.

She hated to tell him but she had to. Sonja turned on the bench, facing directly into his dark eyes. "I'm afraid so."

"She's gone?" He rubbed his head. "Truly?"

"Yes." Tapping her package, she frowned. "I hate to be so blunt, but I have her headstone here and I'm not sure where to put it."

A muscle in his jaw jumped. "I was so looking forward to finally meeting Cora."

Louis Smith had many friends here. Had been well liked at school and church. But his dark eyes, so much like this man's, had always been filled with sorrow after his father's untimely death.

"I'm so sorry." Sonja fisted her hands, inside the snug gloves. "I know you cared deeply for her."

Deeply enough to offer marriage.

They sat in silence while passengers headed off to hail a taxi or were greeted by friends or relatives who'd arrived in their carriages, an entire queue circling the block. Mr. and Mrs. Hood strolled past, arm-in-arm. The telegram operator cast a quizzical glance at her but said nothing as the group walked past by them, leaving the platform.

Sonja blew out a foggy breath. "I know you must be devastated."

Mr. Penwell met her gaze, his forehead bunching. "Where is she buried?"

"In the pauper's field."

His eyes widened and jaw slackened.

"Would you like to see the grave marker?"

"Yes." He swallowed. "Please."

Sonja pulled the paper free from the carved letters on the top of the small stone plaque.

Louis ran his finger over Cora's birthdate. "This is wrong." His face reddened.

"No. It is correct. She was forty-two last month."

He shook his head.

"Yes." Surely Cora hadn't told him otherwise?

Mr. Penwell ran his tongue over the front of his even teeth.

"We celebrated. I made her a Queen's cake with sugared almonds." Although Cora had insisted it was the last birthday she'd see—and her friend had been correct.

"Forty-two, you say?" His dark eyes widened momentarily but then his features settled into a masklike appearance. "Her letters suggested she was much closer to our age."

Sonja frowned. How would he know her age? Unless he was Louis Smith, as Mrs. Welling suspected? "I was expecting you to be closer to dear Cora's age, sir."

Dare she mention the letter she'd sent? Sooner or later he'd know that someone had offered to be a substitute bride for Cora and he'd infer it was Sonja. Now was not the time, though, to make this revelation. And if he was Louis Smith, why the secrecy?

Mr. Penwell stood abruptly. "Thank you, Miss Hoeke. I've just recollected that I have a meeting with the railroad staff upon my arrival and they may be expecting me."

"Certainly." She held out a hand and he assisted her up, a pained smile flattening his lips.

"May I escort you to dinner, once I am settled, so that you may tell me more about Cora?"

Sonja dipped her chin. "Yes. My parents often have their own plans on Friday night, so I don't need to cook."

She'd not mentioned her name. How did he know she was Miss Hoeke? She met his gaze. Although shabby, she'd worn her deerskin gloves—an anonymous gift left for her at church a decade ago Christmas. Gloves she'd suspected had been left by the boy whose father had died.

Louis's gaze followed hers to her hands and settled there. A rosy tint touched his cheeks and then his brown eyes met hers.

Sonja still wore the gloves he'd left for her all those years ago when she, of all the Hoeke daughters, had none—not even a knit pair. When she'd huddled by the woodstove, during Sunday school, he'd slipped away to the coat closet, retrieved the deerskin gloves, and had tucked them into the pocket of her hand-me-down red coat. Every time he'd seen her wearing them, his heart had warmed, as it had earlier at the station. Perhaps he should have lingered, but his emotions bubbled in such turmoil, he wasn't sure he could manage them in public.

Hours after arriving, Louis still sat at his new walnut desk and reviewed in his mind what had happened earlier that day. He leaned back into his heavily padded and upholstered high-backed chair but it offered no comfort. Cora had died. He was a man of his word, and if she'd accepted his invitation, he'd have felt obligated to honor it despite the difference in their ages. But would Cora even have accepted?

Sonja Hoeke, the quiet, studious and sweet girl of fifteen had grown into a beautiful woman in the dozen years since they'd briefly attended the same public school. He'd graduated two years ahead of her. She had at least five older sisters, all beauties and socially active girls, two of whom became engaged and then married while he lived at the County Farm north of town. And this Hoeke sister—not yet married. How was that possible? Her statement that she could only dine out on Friday, because she cooked all week flummoxed him. Her sisters could be observed engaged in all manner of social activities any night of the week. Had her parents become so infirm that they couldn't manage their own cooking anymore? Mr. Hoeke must be in his sixties by now. Was he still a mail carrier? Hadn't Cora said he was?

Louis opened his leather satchel and removed his planner book and well-worn Bible. He could put his pocket

Bible in the desk and bring the family one to the inn. There, in King James' English, he'd find answers. And on the morrow, he'd attend service at the Christian Church. Would the parishioners recognize him as Louis Smith, the scrawny boy from the Poor Farm? With Mr. Welling now gone, rest his soul, who would know that Penwell was his true name?

After a hearty breakfast at the restaurant below the inn, Louis rode out to his old church, looking for answers. So far, the few people he'd encountered in town failed to recognize him. That was a good thing. He needed time. After church, he wanted to talk with the preacher about the situation with Cora. Had a proper service been done? Could she be disinterred and moved to the church cemetery?

Louis entered the building's new addition. As he headed down the hall, his dress broughams tapped out a steady beat on the pine floors. Classes lined the long rectangular corridor, with boys and girls divided by age group—if all was done as when he attended. The children now exited into the hallway. Framed in a doorway stood beautiful Miss Hoeke, dressed in a somber blue dress, a white knit shawl wrapped around her shoulders.

"Good morning, Miss Hoeke."

"Good to see you, Mr. Penwell." Her voice held a tease. "Are you here to be a sheep or a shepherd?"

"For?"

She arched a light brow at him. "Our Christmas pageant, of course."

He shrugged. "I'd prefer narrator. I'm told I have a booming voice."

"Well, we already have an excellent orator. Ronald has volunteered." She gave him an appraising glance, a smile tugging on her lips. "Should I ask our seamstress to stitch you up a fluffy covering or a burlap robe?"

"Not burlap." He feigned scratching at his arms. "I itch just imagining it."

"But, sir, they are free from the feed store in town, and we must utilize them lest we not receive the Gibson's good offer again!"

This was the girl he remembered who'd read from Mark Twain at a school event, and whose vocal inflexions and accents brought the story to life, along with her animated expression as she narrated the tale.

Other Sunday school teachers meandered down the hall toward them. He wanted to ask Sonja about Cora's class before they were interrupted. "Were you just teaching the fourth grade girls in Cora's class? Have you taken over or are you substituting for now?"

She blinked rapidly. "Often the proprietress of the County Farm wouldn't allow Cora and the others to come into town."

"Why?"

"Mrs. Geisig, claims she needs the…inmates…at home." Sonja detested that word, but perhaps it did explain their actual circumstances. "In fact, I fear she didn't allow them to attend today, either."

How dare she refer to that oppressive environment of the Poor Farm as a home? Why had Cora lied? Or had she stretched the truth? He clenched his fists but then forced his fingers open. "I may have read more into her letters than was intended. Cora indicated that she helped teach the Sunday school class."

Sonja cocked her head and her brows knit together. "Cora did indeed help me out. I tried to keep her near me with the girls. She seemed to understand their lessons better than she did some of the sermons."

"Oh?"

She ran her tongue over her upper lip. "You see, Cora only recently accepted the Lord as Savior."

Heavy-heeled footfall sounded behind him.

"Good morning, Sonja." A petite redhead gave him the once-over, which should have flattered him. But, if he was correct, that was Letitia, who'd been a terror in school. Even though he'd tried to protect her from taunts, she had always acted hostile toward him.

"Lettie, this is Louis Penwell, the new railroad manager for our fair town."

"Mr. Penwell, pleased to meet you." The pretty woman extended her hand and for a moment he wondered if he was supposed to kiss it. While women out west had taken to shaking hands, often vigorously, he didn't recollect them doing so here in the Midwest. But times were changing, were they not? He gently grasped her hand and then released it.

"I'm Letitia Brown, and I'd best get to my pew before Mama and Papa come looking." She gave a little wave and scurried off down the beeswax-scented corridor.

"Are you coming into service?" Sonja's soft, sage green eyes met his.

"Yes." He'd need to speak with the minister afterward, too. His time in the Word gave him more questions than answers. He'd seek out godly counsel. The name listed on the sign inside the corridor showed a new pastor at the church since Louis had attended.

"My parents were both unable to attend today." She offered a warm smile. "Would you care to sit with me?"

Louis took her arm in his and escorted her down the hall. Having Miss Hoeke on his arm felt like the most natural thing in the world. He straightened his shoulders.

The pretty blonde laughed and pointed at a poster board on the wall, promoting the upcoming Christmas pageant. "Look at the sheep the children have been adding around the manger scene."

They paused and she counted aloud, finally stopping at eight.

"So, you have all those sheep volunteers already. How about I'll be one of the shepherds? I don't see any of those drawn in, and I'm very handy with a pencil."

After pulling her arm free, Miss Hoeke opened her reticule and offered a short pencil. "Display your artistry, sir, and confirm your claim."

He pressed a hand to his chest in mock dismay and then bowed low. "I am humbled by your lack of faith in my abilities." When he straightened, she covered her mouth with her hands, laughing.

"I can see that you have a dramatic bent, Mr. Penwell. Now demonstrate your artistic skills."

With a flourish, he pulled back his jacket over his left hip, resting his hand there, and then raised his right arm. In a dash, he drew a rudimentary stick figure holding a cane.

She rolled her eyes.

"I didn't want the children to feel bad about their own drawings." He winked. "Or I'd have created a masterpiece of a shepherd."

Blonde curls bounced as she slowly shook her head. "I've heard that one before from students claiming they don't want to outshine their Sunday school classmates."

He raised his hands in surrender. "*Mea culpa.*"

Mea culpa. Guilty.

Louis Penwell was droll and adorable. Was he the type of man to see humor in the letter she'd written, offering to be his substitute bride? She prayed the letter would get lost in its return from the West. Nibbling her lower lip, she had to be honest with herself. She was drawn to this man. And guilt niggled at her as he drew her arm back atop his, her palm resting in his broad, warm hand. This felt right, no matter what logic argued.

"May I escort you into the sanctuary?" Although the long corridor divided into two options, Louis seemed to know exactly where he was heading.

She looked up into his dark eyes. For a moment, she was fifteen, again, gazing up at the new boy in church. The slender, handsome youth, who had come to services alone. "Louis?" Her voice quavered.

His smiled faltered. "Yes?" His Adam's apple bobbed above his striped bow tie, the twin starched inverted triangles of his white shirt collar remaining motionless.

Blinking away her apprehension, Sonja examined the man's face. Louis Smith Penwell—why hadn't she put those names together before? Louis Smith, the boy whose father had drowned, had been placed at the County Farm when the Smith home was destroyed by the fire in Salt River. Was it possible that this railroad man was a descendant of the Louis Smith Penwell—the famous politician and inventor from Virginia? Now wasn't the time to ask. The Sunday school classes had emptied out, and only the tardiest churchgoers would be entering the building now. "We best get going."

With no hesitation whatsoever, Mr. Penwell steered her toward the sanctuary. At the door, their deacon, Mr. Stewart, greeted them warmly, glancing between her and Mr. Penwell, a line forming between his sandy eyebrows. Past him in the last seat, his pretty wife, MaryBeth, swiveled to look at them. Arching a brow she also stared at Louis and then at Sonja before offering her a wide knowing smile.

Oh no.

Oh no. Here he was again after all these years.

Louis swallowed as he attempted to guide Sonja to an empty pew in the back right row, opposite the Stewart's pew. Instead, she pointed out her family's normal spot—the same even after a decade. Aware of the many eyes on them, Louis straightened and assumed his railroad's man posture as he pretended a confidence he lacked at this moment. Murmurs rose, and he was certain he'd overheard the words "Louis" and "Smith."

Their posteriors had no sooner settled upon the pine pew seats when the pastor entered. *Thank you, sweet Jesus.* Louis pulled out his linen handkerchief and wiped the perspiration that had formed on his brow, despite the chill in the building.

Reverend Mathews possessed a humble, yet powerful, spirit. His sermon on living for God, and not for possessions, hit Louis like a wave of a Great Lakes storm of immense magnitude. No, Louis hadn't worked hard for goods, *per se*, but his intention had been the same—to provide material wealth and position to ensure he'd never suffer his father's fate, nor would his future family. The family he'd not yet started even as he approached thirty. Yes, there had been lady friends, but none had understood him like the widowed correspondent who'd resided in the same Poor House he'd escaped from years earlier. Now Cora was with the Lord. At least she had come to know the Lord through their letters and through her friendship with Sonja. And through this church.

"Christmas is coming soon, friends." Reverend Mathews gestured in Sonja's direction. "Miss Hoeke is heading up the pageant this year, and we still need volunteers. And donations, too. Would you stand and tell us more, Sonja?"

A blush washed her lovely features but Sonja rose, brushing back a tendril of blonde hair from above the lacy neckline of her blouse. "Yes, well, our program theme this year is about coming home for Christmas."

Chills shot up his arms from beneath his wool jacket.

Sonja rotated slowly to face the other side of the room and then looked over her shoulder. "With so many lost from the recent illness, we have former members who are returning to…" She wiped away a tear. "To visit their loved ones."

Living and dead. He'd not yet visited his father's unmarked grave, but today he would. And he'd check with the sexton tomorrow about getting a marker made. And he'd speak with both the minister and the sexton about having both Father's and Cora's remains moved.

The small bustle of Sonja's gray and black striped ensemble pressed too near his face, as she rotated, so Louis scooted over on the pew, engendering some amused glances from the men seated with their wives in the pews ahead of them.

"So, we'll need more of the marvelous baked goods our ladies make—including my famous gingerbread, of course." She bobbed a little curtsey as laughter erupted.

"We'll need the dentist there, then!" A portly man called out and winked at Louis.

Sonja laughed as she raised a hand. "This year, I promise I shall allow Mother to make it instead."

"Oh no, ma'am!" A deep voice called out.

Louis turned to locate the speaker.

Although he possessed less hair on his head and more on his face now, the dentist, who'd been brand new in Salt River when Louis and his father had arrived, stood and grinned. "I could use a little extra business before Christmas. Got new skates to buy for the children."

Louis counted six children with various shades of red hair, and the man's wife, her belly round with another blessing. The dentist sat, and Louis couldn't help chuckling, too, as he faced the pastor, again. Although he'd not known Sonja well, other than admiring her from a distance at school and church, he had partaken of her baking efforts. The younger boys had used the biscuits in a game where they tossed them in a basket from various distances.

Sonja tapped Louis shoulder. "I have a potential volunteer shepherd, and he's new to town."

A titter rippled through the room, and Louis sensed movement behind them as well as viewed people in front of him craning their necks.

"So, if Mr. Penwell can help with our pageant, then let him be an example to others who have hesitated to sign up." Sonja slowly rotated and Louis remained arched away from her bustle as she turned. "Thank you!"

As she sat, Sonja arranged her full skirts around her, perching herself near the edge of the seat, her bustle preventing her from sitting fully back against the pew. He slid a little closer.

Once Reverend Mathews completed the service and dismissed them, Louis rose and assisted Sonja up. Seated the third row from the front, he hoped to avoid some of the comments he'd surely receive. He wouldn't lie. He was the Louis Smith they'd known, but his father, a drunkard and gambler, had dropped his distinctive surname of Penwell as his life became more dissolute. Louis, himself, wouldn't have known his own last name had his mother not told him when she was dying. And Mother had said, "Your father is a good man. Forgive him."

Of course he had forgiven the man who'd loved him and taught him so many things—when he was sober. But forgiveness had taken many years.

From the front, Mr. and Mrs. Thomas Wenham, who'd fed him more times than Louis could remember, moved toward them as Sonja maneuvered out of their pew and into the aisle. He squeezed her elbow. "Excuse me, Sonja."

Louis slipped from the pew and joined the Wenhams before Sonja could overhear any conversation. For years, the notion of returning to Salt River, now Shepherd, had been the stuff of his nightmares. Yet now, the love, the welcome, the homecoming was palpable in this church. With these people.

Gray now streaked Thomas's temples and threaded through Fanny's hair. "Louis, is it you? Louis Smith?"

"It's me—Louis Smith Penwell." When he held out his hand, the farmer grasped it firmly and pulled Louis into a quick embrace.

"Well, I'll be!" Mr. Wenham released him and then gestured for someone behind Louis to join them. "Martin, it's Louis."

Both Thomas Wenham and Martin Gade had been in the boat with Louis's father the fateful day they'd headed out with the maple syrup and ended up sinking instead. Mr. Gade, the most prosperous of the men, had helped those he could. But he couldn't bring Father back nor could he support an almost fully grown young man at his own table. So off Louis had gone to the Poor Farm.

Martin's swarthy complexion paled as his dark eyes scanned Louis's face. "Penwell? Not Smith?"

"Yes, sir."

"Well, I'll be. You look like you've done well for yourself, son. We've been praying for you all these years."

Fleeting movement in the back of the room caught Louis's eye. A slender, almost wraith-like woman attired in a long black coat, her hair covered by a snug hat to which was affixed a heavy veil, glided past the minister without pausing to address anyone.

He glanced quickly at Sonja, waiting for him in the aisle. She followed his gaze.

"Excuse me. I see someone I must speak with…" Louis slipped away as the two men gaped at him. If he didn't catch her now, how would he know if it was *her*—the woman he'd seen only a handful of times before? And always at critical times in his life.

Chapter Five

Sonja tugged her heavy winter skirt aside and followed Louis as he worked his way through the congregants. The raven-like woman he'd pursued pulled something from her reticule—a paper wrapped square—and quickly slid it onto a low shelf in the vestibule. She exited the building while Louis wove through the labyrinth of people, and then stopped by the preacher.

As Sonja made her way to Reverend Mathews, she caught the distinctive scent of incense or some other Middle Eastern fragrance. She paused. Once, a missionary had brought frankincense and myrrh to her Sunday school classroom, and this fragrance smelled similar.

Reverend Mathews shook Louis's hand heartily and glanced between him and Sonja. "Is this your young man, Sonja? Your father had promised me a Christmas wedding, and now, here is Mr. Penwell!"

She felt the color drain from her face. When Louis met her gaze, his dark eyes held only admiration. Then, slowly, his expression altered to disappointment.

He sees the shunned, unloved girl I've been. Her heart sank.

"I'm afraid not, pastor, but I'll explain to you later, in private."

Compassion shone in the minister's eyes and then a flicker of devilment. His lids lowered slightly over his green eyes and Reverend Mathews chuckled. "You two let me know if that changes, all right? I've got my wedding ceremony all ready for you, Miss Hoeke."

Louis laughed. "Thank you, Reverend Mathews. We'll be sure to do that. Also, if you don't mind, I need to speak with you about a private matter."

"Are you coming with Sonja to the rehearsal?"

"Yes, sir."

"How about we'll chat after that?"

"Fine. Thank you."

Sonja beamed at him, as though he'd just offered her a splendid gift. Was his time that special to her? What a blessing it would be to have her look at him like that every day.

He took her hand and guided her to the coat closet, where a line had formed. A muscle in his cheek jumped. He wasn't very good at waiting. But patience was a virtue he'd benefit from acquiring. One by one, the congregants retrieved their winter coats, donned them and their hats and gloves, and then left. Finally Louis lifted Sonja's coat from a heavy wooden hanger and assisted her into the too-short fur garment.

His heart tugged as she pulled out the deerskin gloves and tugged them on. Tomorrow, he'd order her a new pair—lined calfskin gloves from Detroit.

Sonja tapped his coat sleeve. "Who was that woman, Louis? The lady in the mourning gown?"

"Hmmm?" He pulled out his pocket watch, a fine piece with engravings of bear and deer on it—one of his first purchases as a railwayman.

"The woman in black you tried to catch up with."

He exhaled a whoosh. "I don't really know. But I've seen her several times." At his college graduation. As soon as he'd received his diploma, he'd spied her stand and slip from the auditorium.

The blacksmith, Mr. Campbell, and his wife joined them. "Louis? Louis Smith?"

Louis pivoted and extended his hand. "Actually it's Louis Penwell, Louis Smith Penwell."

The couple frowned. "Not Smith?"

"My father chose to use that name, sir."

"Why?" Sonja hadn't stopped the question from slipping out and couldn't take it back. When Louis had helped her into her coat, he'd sent a jolt through her when his hands had brushed her shoulders. Maybe that was why she couldn't think straight. Even now she trembled at the thought of his touch. Heavens, how would she be able to conduct her rehearsal properly?

Louis ran a hand through his hair and offered a slight smile to each of them. "I'll explain it all, but trust me, there is nothing nefarious in it—other than having a father who regularly gambled away our funds and moved us from one place to another before he'd finally found Jesus—here, in this place, before he died."

"Praise God for that, then." Mrs. Campbell tugged on her husband's arm. "And we both welcome you back."

"Yes, welcome, Louis." Mr. Campbell grinned. "We best get on our way—don't want to keep that good roast waiting."

Mrs. Campbell laughed and the two strode off, arm in arm.

Sonja needed to focus on her schedule. "I hate to rush, Louis, but I do need to partake of a quick lunch before I return for practice."

"Lunch with me, of course?" He winked at her. "As we are betrothed, according to someone."

Had he received the letter? Had he guessed? Or did he mean Reverend Mathews' comments? She sighed. "My father has offered me in marriage to any unmarried man in the town."

"What?" the small lines around his eyes deepened. "And whom have you chosen?"

A stranger in South Dakota who'd proposed to my best friend. "I'm afraid I'll be assigned to a new postal position soon, so it doesn't matter. I'll be moving."

Not if he had anything to do with it. Sonja Hoeke would become *Sonja Penwell*, if God willed it. "I'm afraid I won't have a carriage at my convenience until tomorrow. Come, let me walk you to the restaurant at the inn."

"Are you sure?" She tipped her head in a most becoming way.

"I insist, and of course I shall pay for our expenses. I'm on an account until my home is finished." A blessing since he had no way to prepare meals.

"The railroad is building you a house?" Sonja wrapped a long, knit, shawl over her beautiful blonde, upswept hair. What a shame—the garment shrouded her beauty and made her appear like an elderly woman. When they were married, he'd send to Detroit for new fancy hats for her. Gloves were one thing—hats another. She must be his wife before he'd outfit her in grand style.

"One of the benefits of this new position." But the inn owner seemed confused when he'd shared this information with him. "They assured me the house would be a grand place."

Sonja cocked her head, the dark shawl slipping against her cheek, contrasting with her ivory complexion. "Louis, there is no new construction. There cannot be—not with winter almost here. And if there were plans—well, most of the men in town would be talking about it."

He stiffened. His supervisor told him the investors arranged for him to have a beautiful new home. Someone tapped on his shoulder. He turned to see the preacher.

"Mr. Penwell?" Reverend Mathews extended a brown paper-wrapped package. "Someone left this for you."

"Thank you." He accepted it.

"Have a blessed day! I'm off to join my family for stewed chicken." The minister patted his flat stomach and grinned. "We'll see you at the end of practice, Sonja."

"Yes, sir."

Mr. and Mrs. Mathews followed them from the building. The preacher didn't stop to lock it, either, despite all the congregants being gone. With Louis's bad experiences in this town, he imagined every door should be locked. Yet, he was being welcomed back with open arms. They descended the front steps, Louis holding Sonja's elbow until they reached the bottom, when she turned toward him.

"Unwrap it." Sonja tapped the parcel. "That woman in black left it on the shelf for you. I saw her."

He pulled at the string that secured the paper. Sonja yanked the paper away, revealing Charles Dickens' *A Christmas Carol*. An envelope's edge peeked out from a third of the way into the book. He opened the marked spot. "This is where Christmas Past begins."

Sonja took the heavy ecru envelope attached to the gift and opened it. She certainly was acting proprietary—like a wife. He couldn't help grinning but wondered what the note said. "I believe that is mine, madam."

Her cheeks flushed. "Miss—not madam."

Not for long. Louis unfolded the note but leaned in toward her as they read.

Christmas past wasn't so horrible—if you only look for the love there. You found it in this place. Let God bring healing.

Memories of laughter and hugs chased each other in quick succession.

Chills raced up his arms and something wet his cheeks. He brushed away the unbidden tears, and turned from Sonja who still gazed with rapt attention at the letter. "Louis, who was that woman?"

"I don't know." She'd been there at the back of the small group for his father's funeral but had slipped away. There at his high school graduation, too. It wasn't until the college graduation that he truly took note.

As they walked, Louis tucked his arm through hers. Would the handsome man be so solicitous when he realized that after his intended, her friend, had died, she'd offered herself as a substitute?

"Here we are." He stopped in front of the restaurant, which covered the first story of the clapboard building that comprised the inn.

As he opened the door, the chilly breeze accompanied them into the well-heated establishment. Wide pine planked flooring was marked by wet boot imprints. Most of the inglenook booths were filled—except the one Sonja's family normally occupied.

Miss Mitchell, the proprietor's youngest daughter, smiled up at Louis, her eyes wide. Although only sixteen, many girls in these parts were already married. "Should I seat you in your parents' booth, Miss Hoeke?"

Sonja cringed. Hearing little Debbie Mitchell call her "Miss Hoeke" only served to emphasize their age differences; Sonja's advanced status as an old maid. "Yes, thank you."

Louis bent and whispered something to Miss Mitchell. He handed her the package and the girl tucked it under her arm. "I'll set it behind the counter, Mr. Penwell."

After they were seated and a menu card offered, Sonja pointed out her favorite of the four selections. "Their venison steak is the best."

He laughed. "I had plenty of wild game meat while out west. I believe it's the chicken and dumplings for me. And plenty of biscuits."

Mrs. Mitchell slid a basket of cornbread and biscuits in front of them. "Believe I heard you beg for our dumplings, sir, is that correct?"

"Yes, ma'am."

"You won't regret it. And Sonja, I'll have your venison out, too."

She shrugged. "Let's make it the chicken and dumplings for me, too."

With eyebrows raised, their waitress turned and headed to the back to the kitchen.

Sonja lifted a cornbread square and placed it on her plate. "I usually have biscuits but I'm going to have the cornbread today."

Louis slathered butter, from a blue crock, onto his biscuit. "Seems you're trying a number of new things."

"Indeed."

"But I'd rather you'd not commit to the one."

She stiffened. Had he received her letter? Had he guessed? Had this man attended service and now invited her to lunch to tell her that while he appreciated her offer, he'd not accept it?

Sonja set the baked good onto her plate. Deborah approached with the coffee pot and poured for them, pushing the creamer in Sonja's direction. She smiled at her, grateful the young woman had known she needed a drink and quickly.

Perhaps he'd best not comment on her postal job. Louis didn't want to push his luck. Or blessings as they may be. He chose to change the topic after seeing Sonja's face blanch. Perhaps he was scaring her with his rushed courtship. Was that what this was? Courtship? With the handful of women he'd courted, all had ceased allowing him to call on them after he'd missed multiple events because of his work. And now he may lose his opportunity with Sonja because of *her* work. God had a sense of irony—that was for sure.

"Sonja." Maybe he should be more formal. "Miss Hoeke…"

She raised a hand. "Please, feel free to continue calling me Sonja. After all, I was a dear friend of your intended, as you mentioned."

His intended? How had she known? Had she read his proposal of marriage? It had arrived *after* Cora's death. Perplexed, he took a bite of biscuit and chewed, but it suddenly lacked flavor. Louis set it down and took a long swig of black coffee. "Why don't we visit Cora's grave together tomorrow?"

He'd have contacted the sexton by then and made arrangements for the move and could share that with her.

"I have to carry my father's route for him."

"Perhaps after?"

She cocked her head at him. "I'll get my chores done quickly after work, and I'll meet you there."

Soon their meal arrived. He surreptitiously watched as Sonja enjoyed her food. She closed her eyes and smiled, as she obviously savored her food. He grinned. This woman enjoyed life. Somehow Sonja had become more like those sisters of hers, who always seemed to be having a gay old time. Sonja relished the moment, as those young women used to do, while she'd trailed after them. He needed to enjoy life more, too. She suddenly opened her eyes and fixed him with a gaze as she ran the tip of her tongue over a bit of gravy that clung to her perfect lips. He swallowed.

"What are you thinking, Louis?"

"I…" He drew in a deep breath and patted his mouth with his napkin, then set it aside. "I was wondering how your sisters are faring."

Blinking at him, she speared a bit of chicken and brought it to her mouth. Then she cocked her head at him as she chewed.

"I remember a beautiful girl who followed her sisters around and they treated her as though she was a stray cat."

A spark flared in Sonja's green eyes. She set her fork on the ironstone plate. She huffed a laugh. "Cora was more a sister to me than my own were. Each has gone off, and the only time Mother and Father hear from them is when they need something." A few heads swiveled to look in their direction as Sonja's voice rose.

Louis leaned in and covered her hand, tapping the tabletop with his own. "I'm sorry. You deserve better. And I'm glad our mutual friend was a blessing to you, as she was to me."

Sonja impaled another piece of meat with her fork. "Can you believe my own sister would take my dog away after her last visit? My pet."

"What?"

"She said her children needed Darren more than I did." She tucked the piece of chicken into her mouth and chewed, glaring at Louis as though he had kidnapped her pooch. She swallowed and then set her utensils aside.

"Darren? Strange name for a dog."

She laughed. "An old beau's name. And believe me— Dar was a better companion than Darren, the man, proved to be."

"Didn't your parents object to your sister running off with your canine?"

"Mother is too busy trying to manage father and his diet. She believes he has diabetes as he's intolerable if he consumes too many sweets—which he does often."

"And your father truly means to have you leave?"

"Yes."

"Why?"

She puffed out a breath. "I can't really say."

Louis's list of things to accomplish just grew. He'd discover her sister's address and retrieve the dog if it was the last thing he did that week. "Which sister did you say had your pet with her now?"

"I didn't say." Sonja tasted her cornbread. Much better than her own.

They both finished their meals, chatting about upcoming events in Shepherd. She'd tactfully omitted anything about the maple syrup run that year, and he was grateful. He didn't like the reminder of how he'd lost his father. Louis paid the bill and then escorted Sonja to the church. They both shivered, as the temperature seemed to have dropped in that short time, as it sometimes did before a snowstorm.

"I do wish I had some real sheepskins we could use for the children." Sonja glanced up at him, her face now covered by the shawl, her voice muffled. "Or shepherd's garb. Even some striped blankets or something."

Louis stopped walking and Sonja did, also. "I may have just the thing at my new office."

"Truly?"

"I brought several Navajo blankets with me in case the stove was cold in there, which it was before the man delivered my wood and we got a fire going."

"That would be marvelous. Do you mind loaning them to us?"

"They are a bit threadbare, but I don't imagine most shepherds would have been dressed in fine clothes, do you?"

She shook her head.

"How about I'll run over and get them?"

Her dubious look reminded him of one his last lady friend wore, right before he'd set out to his office to pick up some records. When he'd later failed to meet her at her parents' home for dinner, their courtship ended before it had really begun.

She tugged at her gloves. "Will you take part in the play?"

"If you need me, I shall." He squeezed her hand and then released it. "The railroad office is just around the corner, and I'll be right back in two flicks of a cow's tail."

"I think you mean donkey's tail—we've no cows in this production, sir." She smiled prettily, and for a dizzying moment he was tempted to kiss her right then and there.

He laughed, regained control of his impulses, then turned and strode toward his new workplace. After two blocks he was a tad winded. Needed to get back on his walking pace again. As Louis drew his key from his pocket, the wind picked up, shooting needles of prickly, cold air through him. He hastily inserted the key into the door lock. It was already unlocked. He hesitated. Who would be inside?

Slowly, he turned the knob and opened the door. Kneeling before his desk, scrubbing the floor, the washerwoman paused. He exhaled, entered the building, and then closed the door behind him.

"Just finishin' up here, sir, eh? Only be but a moment." The woman's drab clothes puddled around her. Her face remained turned away from him, her head wrapped in what appeared to be cotton rags or a large, faded cotton scarf.

"No trouble. I'm simply here to retrieve something, and I'll be out of your way." Strange to have someone here on a Sunday. But Louis hadn't read all his predecessor's notes when he'd been in the office on Friday so he wasn't sure of the schedule. He'd simply settled his own belongings, preparing to work on Monday morning. He was turning over a new leaf. He had to. That new beginning meant allowing time for life. A life that included Sonja.

Louis went to the closet and opened it. Light streaming through a nearby window assisted him as he sought out the blankets. He pulled out the three woven, striped blankets and ran his hand over them. He'd purchased them from a Navajo trader when he'd first moved out west, and they'd kept him warm through many winters.

The door opened and then quickly closed. Louis pulled the blankets against his chest and turned. The cleaning lady hadn't even bidden him goodbye. He exhaled loudly. He hoped she'd not be a problem like some of his previous office servants had been.

While he was here, he'd quickly glance at his schedule for the week and at notes left for him for basic functions, such as when he'd likely see the maid again.

As he approached the desk, his eyes lit upon a paper-wrapped package—identical to the one he'd left at the restaurant. Had the strange woman from church slipped in while the washerwoman was there?

Bending over the wide oak desk, covered with a blotter, he read the writing on the brown paper wrapping. *The Present.*

Swiftly untying the bundle, which felt very much the same size as the Dickens' book, he opened it to discover an identical copy. Although this one had something marking it about halfway through. Scrawled on an index card was the quote, "There's no time like the present." He flipped the card over. Written on the back was, "Don't miss it."

Sonja led the girls through their songs, still awaiting Louis's return. How long could it take to grab some blankets? Finally, she heard the sanctuary doors open and then close. Instead of joining them, he sat on a pew near the back. He laid his new book on his lap and held several striped blankets or serapes in his arms. His eyes were wide, as though shocked. His countenance bore the same affect she'd remembered on his handsome face, as a youth, when his father had died.

When the song was over, Sonja motioned Louis forward. He carried several blankets and offered them to her. "Thank you, Mr. Penwell."

She needed to set the tone and not have her young charges making any inferences about the relationship between herself and Mr. Penwell. But two of the girls had already informed her that their mothers were planning on making a wedding quilt for her and Louis's supposed upcoming wedding. She'd set them straight, but both had giggled as though they knew something Sonja didn't know. *Busybodies in this community—always trying to push people into marriage.* At least her old beau, Darren, had known enough to not succumb to their pushing. Or maybe he had. Maybe they had pushed him away and right into the arms of the young woman from Lansing with whom he'd eloped. She'd never thought Darren and she would wed anyway. Her naming of her black Labrador-shepherd mix was not from spite but fun. Surely that was the reason, wasn't it?

Louis pointed. "Where are your shepherds, Miss Hoeke?"

"I'm afraid my narrator and two shepherds are not here. Perhaps Mrs. Geisig couldn't do without them today." Old biddy probably wouldn't spare the extra hay so the horses could carry them to town. "They weren't at church, either."

"Sorry to hear that."

"Would you care to narrate, Mr. Penwell?"

"Me?"

"You offered earlier, silly, don't you remember?"

He flexed his fingers over the book he still clutched. "No time like the present, is there?"

Chapter Six

A "Merry Christmas, Merry Christmas, Merry Christmas," chorus echoed in Sonja's mind all day as she'd worked her father's mail route. Only one more stop remained for mail delivery on the route—the Poor Farm. Young Mrs. Welling had returned to Mackinac Island and the mail was put on hold. A twinge of sorrow worked through her. Both Cora and sweet elderly Mr. Welling had succumbed to illness. Christmas this year wouldn't be the same. The "Merry Christmas" song ceased its repetition in her mind. If it hadn't been for Louis Penwell, Sonja would be lonely, indeed.

Snug in the fur coat, Sonja ignored the flakes of snow that drifted down—until several fell on her nose and she sneezed. This Christmas could still be a blessed one. She felt it in her soul. The practice had gone beautifully with Louis's narration of the Biblical passage of Christ's birth. And all of her "sheep" and "shepherds" had eaten their cookies in the fellowship hall at their table rather than racing around the building with them. That counted as a great success. She credited Louis's raised eyebrow and his warning glance for keeping her little flock in line during refreshment time. Sonja couldn't help grinning.

As she directed the mare to turn up the rutted lane toward the Poor Farm, she spied movement from the house.

Forgive me, Lord, for thinking so harshly of Mrs. Geisig—there may be a perfectly good reason why the children weren't at church yesterday.

Dark, rectangular boxes or trunks dotted the wraparound porch of the Victorian home. What was going on? Sonja flicked the reins. As she drew closer to the large house, she more clearly discerned luggage and crates of goods. Good quality, chestnut-hued, leather suitcases and trunks covered the entire front expanse. So why would such a person be coming to the Poor Farm? Normally, Iris notified the post office of any new inmates.

The short, round, woman, dressed in a coat buttoned up to her triple chins, emerged through the front door, pulling her brown cap down over her hair and ears.

Clucking her tongue, Sonja urged the mare closer.

A tall, broad-shouldered man with a shock of gray hair exited the house and joined Mrs. Geisig on the porch. Beyond the house, the two gray geldings owned by the farm pulled forward the farm's carriage. Ronald, who'd sometimes performed taxi work with his father before the poor man had passed away, drove the coupe forward, a grim line of determination on his flushed face. He gave Sonja a curt nod as he brought the vehicle to a stop.

After securing the carriage, Sonja approached the duo on the porch, clutching the mail to her chest. "Going somewhere?"

"On a very long trip, dearie!" Mrs. Geisig cackled. "I'm out of this place."

"Out?"

"Leaving! My brother-in-law has come to fetch me home."

"Is everything all right?"

"Fine as goose down, thank you very much." She glanced up at the tall man beside her. "But those brats upstairs are sick with whatever killed Cora and old man Welling."

Sonja sucked in a chill breath at the woman's callous words.

"Ain't Iris's responsibility no more." The man jerked a thumb over his shoulder. "This place has been sold."

"Sold?" Sonja squeaked. She looked up at the two.

"Right." Iris squared her shoulders. "And the woman who bought it—she gave me a bundle of money if I'd move on right away."

"But what about the children?" Sonja finally managed, her voice firmer now as she gathered up righteous indignation.

The former matron shrugged and descended the two porch stairs.

"Did you at least send for the doctor?"

"I'm getting Iris home before she gets sick like them inmates." Mrs. Geisig's brother-in-law frowned as he, too, descended the steps. "I left her here when that woman died, and I regretted it."

Mrs. Geisig extended her hand to Sonja. "I'll have that mail now, thank you."

She clutched it to her chest. "There is only one letter for you, and per postal policy I shan't be allowed to give you the rest."

The woman raised her hand as though to strike Sonja or to at least grab the mail. Backing up a step, she flinched. The man grasped the matron's arm, preventing whatever she intended to do. Mrs. Geisig's round face flushed red.

"Ain't worth it Iris, ya got plenty of cash now." He released his hold. "Take your letter and let's get out of this place."

Quickly finding the one missive belonging to the offensive woman, Sonja thrust it at her and then backed away. "I'm going in to check on the children. Would you at least be so kind as to send the doctor out?"

"Not on our dime, missy, but we'll tell him to come."

This man and Mrs. Geisig should get along just fine.

Several customers crowded around the post office wood stove as a gentleman settled his packages on a table nearby. Louis approached the postal counter, inhaling the mingled scent of lemon oil and woodsmoke. "I'm Louis Penwell, the new railroad man. I've come to collect my personal mail, if you have any."

"Nice to meet ye." Mr. McLaughlin blinked up at him.

If he recognized Louis, the postmaster didn't say. They'd never met, because the Poor Farm matron had made the changes to Louis's mail when he'd come to the house and when he'd left.

"I'm delighted to be here with the railroad, in my new position."

"Congratulations, Mr. Penwell. I hear ye are the new manager." The man's Scottish brogue was almost as thick as Louis remembered.

"Yes, and I'm pleased by what a vibrant town Shepherd is—with the railroad as well as the mills, so active." So altered since he'd lived there a decade earlier.

"Times have changed. We certainly see a lot more mail coming through." Behind them the door chimes jingled.

"I can imagine." There was the feeling in the air of change, of progress.

"Oh! Before I forget—I'd not even affixed any postage yet—ye just missed a lady who paid to have us deliver something to ye via the mail." The post office superintendent scratched his head. "She insisted, even after I explained that yer office was only a wee bit up the street."

The crick in Louis's neck, from poring over the two books the previous evening, stiffened further. "Was it a parcel about this big?" He held up his hands to indicate the size of a book.

The man shook his head then bent and retrieved a large envelope and handed it to Louis. "No, it was this."

No return address. And only "Mr. Louis Penwell" was written on the front, in bold lettering.

"Did she give her name, sir?" It had to be the same mysterious woman who'd brought the books.

"Afraid not." He bent once more and retrieved a slim stack of missives and slid them across the counter to Louis. "Here's yer mail. I noticed one was from here."

"I confess, sir, I did live here previously."

"Ye did?"

"My father used the name Smith, then, as did I."

The man's lips formed a sympathetic, 'O'. He shook his head. "So sorry, lad. He was a verra good man. Always had a bit of scripture to quote to me."

How could Louis forget all that had happened in this town? Yes, Father had died. But he'd also gone on to heaven. And he'd changed. "He found the Lord here, sir."

The man cleared his throat. "I *ken* some good came of his short time with us, then, despite all the trouble for ye that followed."

"Yes." God had blessed them here, too. Not all had been bad. Behind him, Louis sensed other patrons stirring.

Mr. MacLaughlin tapped the top letter and frowned. "Looks like Miss Hoeke's handwriting to me. Did ye know her, before?"

"Yes, in school and at church—but we were very young then." And she hadn't known his true surname.

"Verra good. She's a sweet lass." McLaughlin tapped the side of his head. "But I ken, ye're already aware of her disposition."

"Indeed."

McLaughlin rapped three times on the countertop. "I'll cancel the request for her transfer to Mackinac Island, son. Dinna worry about a thing. I'll nay have Sonja sent off right when ye have just arrived."

What if Sonja wished to move on in her postal career? Louis remained silent.

The door opened behind him again, and then closed, bells jingling to announce the new arrival. One of the customers called out, "Good day, Doc."

Louis swiveled to see the physician standing there, face pale.

"Doctor Queen, I've got your mail right here." Mr. MacLaughlin retrieved a pile of missives tied with string.

"I'm here for Penwell." The doctor raised his arm and pointed to the door. "I think he'll want to come with me."

Sonja stirred the simmering kettle of chicken broth as carriage wheels turning announced Ronald's return from town. Shortly, she heard him stumble up the back steps. He lurched into the kitchen, trembling.

He wiped sweat from his brow. "Miss Hoeke, Iris's brother-in-law stopped at the physician's office, but he wasn't there. He left a note."

The young man slumped onto a wood stool by the wall and unbuttoned his coat. "I'll hang this in a minute. But I'm so hot."

"Straight to bed with you!" Sonja aimed her ladle toward the hallway. "Do you need help?"

"No." But when he stood, Ronald's legs looked like they might give out. He removed his jacket, swaying.

Sonja strode to him, wrapped an arm around his waist, and slung his arm over her shoulder. "Come on."

They stopped to hang the threadbare garment, damp from snow, on the coat tree in the hallway.

Heat radiated off the young man much like the cook stove emitted. Like the other residents, he possessed a raging fever. "I'm just weak, is all."

"You're sick." They took several steps toward the stairs. The scent of chicken and herbs overpowered the odor of the dried flowers that Mrs. Geisig had left behind.

He drew in a deep breath. "We've not been fed since two days past."

What kind of monster treated people that way? Sonja clenched her jaw. She wanted to scream in outrage at Iris Geisig. "Let's get you upstairs. I'll pour you some water. And soon I'll be up with some broth."

His stomach growled as they began to mount the stairs.

"If you can keep water down, then I'll give you some crackers."

"Good."

Did she imagine it, or did Ronald seem to be leaning less on her now? "Thank you for putting the horses up. I don't know how you managed."

"God," he murmured. "Only God."

Yes, God was here with them. Tears pricked her eyes but she beat them back with her eyelashes. It wouldn't do for Ronald to see her weeping.

Once upstairs and in his room, the young man sat on his bed and looked down at his feet. Sonja bent, undid his work boots, and pulled them off. He sighed and she looked up.

"No one has done that for me since my Ma died." Ronald's gaze went to his small dresser, atop which a tintype of a young woman gaze in solemnity at the camera.

Those blasted tears threatened again, and Sonja let them chase down her face and fall to the pine floor as she tugged Ronald's damp wool stockings free. "One day, your wife will help you." If he lived. *Dear God, hadn't you just this morning promised me a merry Christmas?*

"Miss Sonja?" His thick voice sounded like Cora's had, when she'd become more ill.

She sniffed as she removed the second wool sock. "Yes?"

"I think I'll just take my suspenders off and sleep in my clothes until the doc gets here, okay?"

Sensing his embarrassment, and suddenly feeling her own, Sonja wiped at her face and stood. "Agreed." She went to the washbasin and found the pitcher beside it, a quarter full. She poured Ronald a glass and brought it to him. She'd need to pump some more and bring it up to all of them, as the girls' pitchers were also getting low.

After he'd gotten beneath his covers, Sonja exited the room, leaving the door slightly ajar. She returned to the kitchen and went to the sink, grateful for the indoor pump, which some homes, including her own, lacked. After plucking a clean jug from the drainboard, she filled it and returned to the hallway. The matron had removed all the framed pictures that had once lined the hallway—bucolic scenes of countryside that in no way reflected life in this house, on this farm.

Two hours later, fatigue hovering over her, Sonja carried up yet another pitcher of cool, fresh water. Wall sconces, lit on her last trip up, cast eerie shadows on the stair treads. After rapping on the first door on the right, she entered the Finnish girl's sickroom. A single kerosene lamp cast a pool of light near the restless girl, whose bedcovers were once again entwined around her thin limbs.

Sonja moved to the bedside and pressed a hand to Liisa's forehead. She was burning up, still. Sonja poured water into the basin. Then she dipped a cloth in water, and dabbed the child's brow. No curtains or wallpaper softened the room. Outside the mullioned windows, the sun dipped low over the tree line. How long until someone came from town? She'd been waiting for two hours, dividing her time between the three patients. God, don't let this child die when she's come so far. Only to have found her father and her brother had died in a lumber camp accident. Those blasted tears filled Sonja's eyes again.

"I'd like to bring up some more broth for you, Liisa." She raised the young girl's head and held a glass of water to her pale lips. "And I want you to try a few crackers."

The girl pressed her eyes shut as if in affirmation.

"I'll be back in a little bit." She had to get some kind of nourishment into them. Ronald had finished a half bowl of soup, with her assistance. They were so weak, how could they fight this illness?

Louis and Dr. Queen discussed Mrs. Geisig at length on their way to the Poor Farm. But he'd not shared with the physician that the Poor Farm property had been deeded to himself by an anonymous benefactor. While waiting at the man's office, Louis had opened the large envelope left for him at the post office. Enclosed had been the property title to the *last place* on earth he'd ever want to own. Someone had a twisted sense of humor. And that morning, he'd received confirmation that no building permits had been sought to construct a new home for him.

He'd not read his other missives, but would do so later, once he and the doctor ascertained the severity of the illness at the Poor Farm. The letter that the postmaster indicated was from Sonja—was it the reply to his invitation to Cora to be wed? Did the young woman know he'd impulsively asked Cora out of desperation to have a mate when he was given his new promotion? What if his pen pal had survived? What if she'd accepted him? And then he'd arrived and become reacquainted with Sonja?

"Last time I was out here was to check on Cora. I understand you were her writing correspondent—a pen pal of sorts?" The doctor directed his black horses to turn onto the country lane, which was dusted with snow.

"Yes. She was a sweet woman who shared the love of the railroad. She'd lost her husband and ended up in desperate straits. But she never lost her kind heart." Louis pressed his spine against the seatback as the horses maneuvered the turn.

"Cora told me that she hoped one day you'd come visit her." Dr. Queen clucked his tongue as the geldings entered the roadway.

"As did I." Louis tugged at the scarf around his neck, holding the front of his rocking seat with his other hand. "Though, in truth, I had no idea I was being sent back here by the railroad. I'd assumed my promotion was where I lived in South Dakota."

Louis turned to gage the doctor's reaction. The physician's rueful smile was broken by a curt laugh. "Did you know Cora wished for you to meet Sonja?"

Redirecting his gaze to the road ahead, Louis shrugged. "I don't believe she knew that we'd already met during our youth."

"Is that correct?"

Dr. Queen hadn't been practicing in the area when Louis had resided in what had later become the town of Shepherd.

"I never mentioned to Cora that I'd lived here. We, that is, I…" He swallowed back the loss he'd experienced. "…lived here for only a little over a year."

They'd first begun corresponding right after her husband had died. He'd seen her letter to the editor of his favorite railroading magazine. He had sought out the correspondence to comfort a widow and share their love of the railroad—for Cora still did enjoy all things related to the railway, despite having lost her husband to it.

"Your letters were a light in her life. But maybe not for the reasons you might think."

A rut in the road jostled Louis and he stiffened.

The doctor cleared his throat. "Cora shared that she believed you and Sonja would be a perfect match. And once she'd accepted the Lord as Savior, Cora prayed that somehow you'd meet her friend."

Louis puzzled over these comments. Had his friend, his pen pal, embellished some of her recent comments about her activities to test the waters as far as Sonja? Was she about to make an introduction by mail? Cora never had implied anything about seeking a romantic relationship, herself, but he'd offered out of friendship, necessity, and the desire to remove her from the Poor Farm.

"Forgive me for overstepping the bounds of professionalism." Dr. Queen kept his gaze focused forward as a light breeze kicked up. "I thought you might wish to know."

"Thank you." His burdens suddenly lightened even as a gust of wind sent snowflakes pummeling into his face and he ducked.

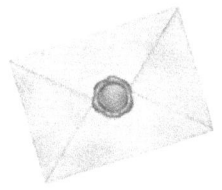

Chapter Seven

*D*esperate to improve her broth and tempt the invalids' appetites, Sonja stood at the stove and added more of what little garlic she'd found and some pepper and parsley. Sampling it, she grimaced. Too much salt, still.

Through the kitchen windows, white snowflakes flurried down, visible in the twilight as the physician's carriage came into view. Her heartbeat escalated. Help had arrived, thank God. As the two bay mares drew to a stop a tall man jumped down and opened the doors to the carriage house. The gig was soon maneuvered into the outbuilding.

Before long, the back door creaked open and then slammed close. The men stamped their feet.

"I'm here in the kitchen!" she called out.

"Going upstairs, Miss Hoeke!" Dr. Queen's baritone voice boomed as he popped his head into the kitchen and unbuttoned his coat.

"I'll be up in a minute, Doc." Louis pulled the physician's coat off and returned to the hallway, where a coat rack stood.

Sonja tossed in a handful of parsley then stirred the soup with a huge wooden spoon she'd found in a drawer. From the looks of things, very little real cooking had gone in the place for several days—just as Ronald had said. Would the young man pull through? Would his college dreams be fulfilled? Would her suggestion that one day his wife would help him with his boots come true?

Louis Penwell entered the cavernous room, and her heart flipped. "Thank God you've come."

"And thank God you were here, Sonja, for the residents." His dark eyes grew even blacker as he took two steps closer to her, then stopped, only inches away.

Her heartbeat sped up. With all those sisters and brothers-in-law, she recognized what *that look* meant. Sonja turned and dropped the spoon into the heavy pot, afraid of what she saw in his eyes. But when she turned back around, Louis hadn't moved. Instead, his gaze danced over her features as he looked at her hair, her eyes, her nose, before settling on her mouth and lingering there. He was thinking about kissing her, and she wanted that kiss, too. Trying to catch her breath, she took one step backward but he caught her by the arm.

"Don't burn yourself on that stove."

He grabbed her elbows, holding her fast. Only the thinnest rim of brown remained around his dark pupils. Tiny lines at the corners of his eyes reminded her of how much time had passed since they'd first met. His lips beckoned her even closer.

Footfall descended the stairs and Louis backed up, gently tugging her in his direction, away from the stove. In a moment the doctor joined them.

"Everything okay?"

"Fine." Except he'd almost kissed Sonja right here in the place he'd hated most—at the farm he now owned—while the occupants, upstairs, lay ill. "Why don't we bring up a little soup, if it's all right?"

"Yes." Sonja's breathless, single word caused him to inhale sharply. One day soon, he'd ask her to marry him and that would be the word he wished to hear.

Louis's world had to have gone off kilter. His organized world, in his job, seemed as distant as South Dakota.

"Sonja, can you fill a couple of mugs?" Dr. Queen's voice held a gravity that made Louis's heart twinge. Unspoken words seemed to hang in the air.

"First, let me add a little water to the broth."

In a few moments, Louis followed Dr. Queen upstairs, carefully holding a mug steady.

When they entered Ronald's room, the young man struggled to get up onto his elbows. The kerosene lamp in the corner cast a pool of light at the bedside, where a small tray-table sat, holding an empty glass and bowl. Louis moved closer.

"We brought you more soup, Ron. And I hope you'll not use this method next time to get out of your oratory obligations." He winked at the youth. "I had to utilize my own rusty skills from my college speech classes to substitute for you."

Behind him, he sensed that the woman he loved had joined them, but he daren't move lest he spill the contents of the mug. Sonja came alongside him, efficiently removing the detritus from the tray. "I'll take all the dishes downstairs and get them washed."

Dr. Queen moved to the other side of the narrow single bed. "Sonja, please boil the water to full roiling for the rinse water."

"I'll come down to pour it for you." Louis didn't want her getting scalded—not after his romantic behavior almost resulted in her getting burned. "Please don't attempt that yourself."

After Ronald was examined, they'd checked on Liisa, who spoke remarkably good English despite her recent arrival from Finland, and then the other girl, Joanna. When finished, Dr. Queen carried his leather satchel into the hallway and set it on a narrow half-oval table, above which a dark, empty circle contrasted with the faded burgundy flocked velvet wallpaper illuminated by wall sconces. "Looks like Iris Geisig even ran off with the mirrors in this place. The board isn't going to like this one bit."

The county board. Louis hadn't considered that now he must answer to them. If he continued to keep this house as a Poor Farm. Which he wasn't sure about. He pulled his handkerchief from his pocket and wiped the sweat from his brow. "I'll stay with the sickest one."

"That would be Joanna." Dr. Queen stroked his chin. "She needs someone with her. In case…"

"All right." Louis cut off the doctor's words. The patients didn't need to hear any dire predictions. "It will take some time for Sonja to get a huge pot of water at a full boil. So I'll stay with Joanna for now and then go help Sonja."

The doctor nodded solemnly. "Not much else I can do here now, Mr. Penwell. I'll be heading back to town."

Louis cringed. The man was leaving them? What if the inmates died? Louis was contemplating the very words he hadn't wish uttered.

Dr. Queen opened his leather bag and removed packets of medication. He handed them to Louis. "One per patient, dissolved completely in a cup of warm water; every few hours until tomorrow night."

"Is that all that can be done?"

"Keep them as comfortable as you can but don't let them get chilled."

Dr. Queen descended the stairs, physician's case in hand.

Louis entered Joanna's room—his old room. He shuddered, as he had earlier when they'd entered. The young woman slept, an arm thrown across her head. Dr. Queen had given her medication earlier. *Dear God, let it work.* Louis set several of the medication packets on top of the monstrous bureau, stained black and carved with what appeared to be snakes—but they might actually have been vines. As a young man, imprisoned here, the carvings seemed to writhe together. He shivered at the recollection of his horrid nights stuck in the room. That piece would be burned for firewood now that Louis owned the place. The foreboding chest of drawers had dominated this room, where he'd once slept for three hundred seventeen nights, all marked off on the back of the piece with a pocket knife.

On impulse, Louis pulled the heavy bureau away from the paneled walled and ran his finger down the back right side. His fingertips hit the grooves and he counted the indentations. They were still there.

God, what am I doing here? Why me?

Dr. Queen entered the kitchen, his coat donned and hat on. Sonja stood by the large cookstove, stirring her secret cider remedy. Scents of chicken broth and apple cider mingled in the steamy room.

The physician tucked his case under his arm. "I'll be back in the morning."

Sonja ladled out spicy apple cider for him, into a mug. With cinnamon, ginger, nutmeg, and cloves, this mixture had helped Cora breathe easier. It was also very tasty. She'd found the spices tucked far back in the cabinet, behind an almost-empty sugar bowl. "Take a cup with you for the road, Dr. Queen."

He accepted the hot cider. "Thank you. I'll check on the horses before I leave and make sure they've got food and water."

"I can do that. Or perhaps Louis can."

"No, I have to go out anyways and it shan't take me long." He stood there, appraising Sonja. "Young woman, you may have saved these inmates' lives. Now we give them into God's hands."

Hours later, exhausted, but unable to sleep, Sonja finally closed down the kitchen and went upstairs to the room where she'd sleep, carrying a bayberry scented lamp. Quietly, she made her way to the northwest bedroom, which was surprisingly large. But this grand house had originally been built for a prosperous farmer. The bedroom would have been filled with furniture and included a portion of the room for a cradle. Who would occupy this room now? Would a happy baby ever coo in this place?

As she searched for bedsheets, Louis's blazing eyes kept intruding on Sonja's thoughts. And now he was only several rooms down the hall. She should offer to remain up with Joanna. What had the doctor been thinking, leaving him there with her? She blinked. She should send him back to town. No, it would be too dangerous now, with the snow already having accumulated several inches, if not more. She huffed out a sigh. Tongues would wag, but there was nothing to be done.

Bending to look under the former matron's bare bed, Sonja discovered a box of blankets stuffed beneath the bed frame. She pulled them out and gathered them up. They were the wool blankets donated by the church years earlier, but all appeared unused. Sighing, Sonja brought several to the first two bedrooms. Each resident had only one thin quilt. Liisa rested comfortably, as did Ronald—both their brows cool, thank God. She extinguished their lamps.

She returned to the matron's room and considered. Dr. Queen wasn't here now, and she would be alone in Joanna's room with Louis. Obligations and duty first—hadn't that been how she'd been raised? And look what it had gotten her—an old maid about to be run off from town. Hands trembling, she retrieved several more blankets and headed back down the hall.

As she entered Joanna's room, she spied Louis, asleep in a chair. Poor man. His pocket watch lay open in his left hand, a book resting in his lap. She leaned closer to look at the time. Three in the morning. No wonder he'd fallen asleep. He'd mentioned he normally rose well before five o'clock to prepare himself for his day's work.

She moved to the bedside and pressed a hand to Joanna's cheek, which felt clammy. She still fought to throw off her fever. Sonja pulled two blankets over the young woman.

She would put the lamp out before she left, but first she'd cover Louis with the last blanket and remove the book from his lap.

As she drew nearer, she saw that it was yet another copy of *A Christmas Carol*. But while the other two books had been printed years, if not decades earlier, this book appeared fresh from the printing press. Its black leather cover showed no signs of wear. Louis's hands rested in his lap, his head tilted to the side against the heavily upholstered sitting chair. Strands of wavy dark hair lay plastered against his forehead.

Oh no. Was he ill, too?

Sonja pressed her hand to his head, which was warm but not hot.

"Don't!" He grasped her wrist and she tried to pull free as he awoke, his eyes wild with fright. His breath came in gasps.

"It's me, Louis, it's Sonja."

He released her arm. "Sonja?"

"Yes." She knelt at his side and tried to remove the book, but his wide hand came down over hers.

"The doctor gave me this book on our ride out." Louis drew in a deep breath.

"Were the others from him, then?"

"No. He said someone left this for me at his office— along with a note for him."

"How odd." She resisted the impulse to kiss his cheek. What would it feel like with the faint stubble on what was usually a cleanly shaven face? "What was the message?"

Louis shrugged. "It said his wages for the year, as consultant for the Poor Farm, had already been deposited at the bank. And that regardless of any payment from the county, or lack thereof, his medical services to any residents at this address were covered. And that additional funds could be requested via the bank."

"Remarkable." She tapped the book, where a piece of black funeral ribbon protruded from a section near the end. "I'm guessing Christmas future was marked in your book."

"It was." He glanced toward the heavy Eastlake chest of drawers. "And I just had the strangest dream."

"What was it?"

He took her hand in his. "I dreamed that I was buried on this property, beneath that chest, and I was screaming to get out."

Sonja shuddered. "How awful!"

"Yes." He squeezed her hand, sending warmth through her. "I called on God and he brought me a book."

She couldn't help laughing. "Surely not *A Christmas Carol*."

No." He chuckled. "I'm positive it was the Bible."

Joanna moaned and rolled toward them. "Miss Hoeke?"

"I'm here."

The girl's eyes grew wide as she looked at Louis. "Who are you?"

"A former inmate here. But now I'm the owner, it seems."

"What?" Sonja and Joanna's voices merged.

"I'm Louis Smith Penwell, once the inhabitant of this very same room—albeit with several other young people in here with me."

Sonja sighed. "I wish my family could have taken you in, Louis."

"With several young women in the home, I doubt your father would have considered it even once."

"He did. Although only once." She smiled.

Joanna's bleary blue gaze moved between Louis and Sonja. "You two know each other? Isn't Mr. Penwell Cora's pen pal?"

"Yes." Louis ran a hand across his forehead. "She was a good friend to me."

Sonja cocked her head to the side. "To all of us."

The girl flopped back onto her pillow. "I guess her plan worked then."

"What was that?" Sonja settled on the bed, beside her.

"She wished for you two to get together—said if only Sonja were your pen pal, Mr. Penwell, that you'd be married by now, and she would be settled in South Dakota."

Louis's deep belly laugh made Sonja cringe. Was he laughing at her? "Joanna, I believe Cora was correct. But perhaps God needed me back here."

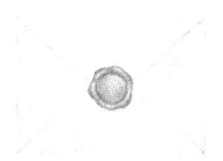

Chapter Eight

*S*o much had happened in the past week, Sonja felt like her head might spin off. Rolling up her last pair of stockings, she wedged them into her grandmother's old trunk. How had the Hoeke family felt crossing an ocean to begin a new life? Sonja's every nerve was on edge, and she was merely moving outside of town.

Her mother knocked on the open door before she entered. "Reverend Mathews is downstairs."

"Oh?" Father had threatened to force a marriage between her and Louis, despite Dr. Queen's arguments that Father was overreacting to the news that the two had spent the night at the Poor Farm together.

"Reverend Mathews will drive you out to the farm. He needs to discuss the plans for the pageant with you. Seems there is to be a larger reception this year."

Sonja exhaled in relief. "We've so much to be thankful for, despite the losses."

Mother drew closer, bringing with her the scent of violets. "Thank God all those pour souls are healing well."

"Yes." Sonja closed the trunk. "And I'm sure Father will be relieved to have me gone."

"Now, dear, you know he loves you…" Mother's words trailed off as her father's footsteps lumbered down the hall.

"He's going to carry your belongings out for you. See how helpful he can be?"

Indeed, since he was getting rid of her. But Sonja bit her tongue and forced a smile.

Louis had read the letter—the response to his proposal to Cora—three times. How could this be? Why would a beautiful, intelligent, and delightful woman such as Sonja Hoeke have offered to become his substitute bride for Cora? On the other hand, how had he become so desperate that he would offer marriage to his pen pal, without either of them ever having met? The Louis he'd been, before he'd returned home—and *yes*, this was his home—seemed a different man.

He'd not yet mentioned the letter to Sonja although he'd been tempted to on their many evenings spent together that week. He'd savored every dinner, every walk, every discussion, and even the pageant rehearsals.

That morning, he'd been told by the railroad that his home wouldn't be constructed until spring—if then, which was why no permits had been sought. And he'd been informed that an investor had already given him a home, hadn't she? So the wraith in black had some railway connection. Beyond that, he still didn't know who she was. Neither did anyone in town—only that everything the stranger did was in cash. Just as she'd conducted business in Shepherd—including having his father's and Cora's bodies disinterred and reburied in the church cemetery before he'd had a chance to pay the sexton. He'd described the woman as "poorly dressed, red washerwoman's hands, a mite of a thing—don't see how she could have afforded the cost." The banker flat out refused to discuss the physician's payments as had the lawyer who'd completed the deed's transaction. Both stated that they would lose their payments should they divulge the woman's identity. Furthermore, both men hinted she'd used a "go between," or even several, to conduct her business.

Was she a long lost Penwell relation? Did it matter? What did count was that he was now to endure at least six months in the tiny, dusty room at the inn. He opened the door to the restaurant below. Sonja should be joining him for lunch, before she drove out to the home. It had taken seven church ladies a week to care for the residents and to bring the house in order, even with Sonja directing them. They'd have to hire additional help. How had Mrs. Geisig managed? Why hadn't she reached out and requested the county provide more workers? Had she? The matron who'd ruled him with an iron fist had brought in her brother, who'd wasted no time in meting out punishment for any of the inmates who didn't pull their load around the place. Then, about the time Louis was to depart for college, the two had disappeared—much like Mrs. Geisig had. Louis came back from the fields one day to find a cleaning woman there. She'd given him a letter with his scholarship information in it. A washer woman. A younger version of the woman in his office that Sunday.

Chills went through him and he blinked back moisture. All those years, after that stranger had led him to believe Mr. Welling had sponsored him for college, he realized that that lowly servant must be the same lady who'd been bringing him these gifts since he'd returned. Why? Did it matter? *Thank you Lord, whatever the reason.*

"Mr. Penwell?" Miss Mitchell peered up at him.

"Hmmm?" He'd gotten lost in his thoughts but forced himself to focus on the young woman.

"Your spot is taken, but I've got a booth right next to it."

The private booth, where he'd normally sat, was occupied by a mature couple. They sat deep back in the Inglenook, their voices low as he was seated at the adjoining booth. "Thank you."

"I'll bring your coffee."

He nodded and pressed back against the seat.

A man's voice rose on the other side. "Can you believe it? We're finally free."

"Oh, Martin, don't speak so!"

"It's true."

The couple continued to argue, apparently about their daughter, who was moving out of their house. Was it the Hoekes? He'd yet to meet them.

"It's embarrassing having an old maid for a daughter. Now she'll be where she belongs—out of my home!"

"Please, Martin, don't raise your voice."

Around them, the tables and booths began to fill as workers took their lunch breaks. Louis wanted to stand and shout at the man behind him, but he held his tongue.

"Why couldn't she have been like her sisters?"

The waitress returned. "Mr. Penwell, um, well, I'm afraid we have a slight problem." She pointed to the windows, outside which a man stood, holding a massive Labrador retriever mix on a leash.

Louis clapped his hands together. "Ah, yes, very good—he's come."

Eyebrows raised high, she leaned in. "He can't stay at the inn, sir, you know that."

After he withdrew three bills from his wallet, Louis handed them to the innkeeper's daughter. "One for your inconvenience, one for the man's and the dog's meals out back of the restaurant, and one for the man for holding onto Darren until I can come retrieve him after lunch."

Eyes wide at the amount she'd been offered, Miss Mitchell took the money, stuffed it into her apron and ran outside. He viewed the animated exchange between her and the dog handler through the window. Crossing the street, Sonja approached her pet. A huge grin split her pretty face and she threw open her arms as though to hug the townsman Louis had employed. Sonja stopped when Miss Mitchell shook her head and spoke to her. Sonja's lower lip drooped but then she again grinned and followed the waitress into the restaurant and headed straight for their booth.

The woman he loved, whom he prayed would be his wife, pressed a hand to her chest. The long, ankle-length, green wool coat he'd sent to her home matched her eyes almost perfectly. He'd learned something from the mysterious stranger who'd gifted him. Those unexpected gifts, as well as the present time, were to be savored.

In the Inglenook behind them, the irritating man again began to rant. "How many years have I waited for this day? All our daughters gone, except one."

Sonja blanched.

Louis held out his hand, palm up, across the table. "Is that your father?"

Eyes wide, she nodded.

"I wanted to talk with you about a letter I received." Louis grasped her hand and squeezed it gently. "One letter I received this week I believe is from you."

She pulled her hand free. "I'm sorry, I can explain."

Mr. Hoeke's voice grew louder. "I've got my house back to myself. No infernal daughters taking up space and good money."

Tears trickled down Sonja's fair cheeks, and Louis fished out his handkerchief and offered it to her. She dabbed away the tears. "Louis, I shouldn't have…"

He raised a hand to silence her and then in a voice he hoped the entire restaurant, now hanging on Mr. Hoeke's every word, would hear, announced, "Never have I had the privilege of knowing a more giving, beautiful, and godly woman than you, Sonja Hoeke."

The titters in the room stopped, as did Mr. Hoeke's barrage of words behind them. Sonja's jaw dropped open.

Louis slid out from the booth and rose to his full height. "If you, Sonja, would only show me the great honor of becoming the woman who'd live with me the rest of our lives, I would be the happiest man on earth." He pressed a hand to his chest, reveling in the dramatic proposal that Mr. Hoeke's noxious words had pushed him into.

From the corner of his eye, he saw Sonja's father scoot to the edge of the Inglenook.

"Only say you'll be mine, my love, and I shall seek out your father's approval—once I meet the man who has produced so fine a lady as you."

Next to him, Mr. Hoeke stood, only a tad shorter than Louis. "I'm right here."

To his surprise, the man hustled to his wife's side of the table, assisted her out and presented her to Louis. "This is my wife, Sonja's mother. And the one who should be credited with any good you see in my daughter."

If only Sonja could slide under the table and disappear. *How humiliating.* While Louis was kibitzing with her father and then hugging her mother, she slipped from the booth and ran from the restaurant. She headed straight to the back, where her dog awaited. Her pretty new coat brushed her boot tops. The surprise gift, apparently from her father, had shocked her. Perhaps he'd not sent it after all. And Father's comments in the restaurant had first mortified her and then astonished her. Perhaps mother was right. Maybe his diabetes was the cause of his erratic behavior.

Darren barked happily in greeting and shook his long tail as she approached. The man who'd brought him must have inhaled his food before he departed, for Darren was tied with a rope to a pole, his bowls of water and food barely touched, but an ironstone platter on the step had been emptied by the human who'd been there.

She looked around, but the dog tender was nowhere in sight.

Louis strode up the side alleyway and joined her. "It fits you perfectly." He gestured to the length of her new coat.

"So it was from you?"

"Consider it my engagement gift to you—although I have another."

"Oh, Louis. I'm so embarrassed." She shook her head.

"No need. Your father needed to be reminded of what a treasure he and your mother were losing!"

Sonja sniffed back tears. "So your offer of employment at the Poor Farm came with additional stipulations, did it?"

"Indeed!" He chuckled.

She feigned dismay.

Louis bent and petted her dog's head. "Glad you got back here, big guy."

Patting Dar's back, two tears rolled down her cheeks. "I've missed you so much," she murmured to her dog.

They stood there, their breath forming mist and mingling. In the distance, a train whistle tooted and they startled. Darren barked at the noise and Louis laughed. "That's right, old boy, you tell those railroad men!"

"Speaking of which, how did you get Dar back from my sister?"

"It took a bit of convincing—and a purebred Irish setter—to convince your brother-in-law that you needed Darren at the Poor Farm."

She laughed, too. "He's wanted a setter for hunting for the longest time. I imagine he's over the moon."

Louis rubbed his chin. "I think he was, in fact."

"Thank you." She'd not realized how terribly she'd missed her pet until she had him right there with her.

"I'd be over the moon, too, if you'll say yes to me." His dark eyes twinkled, and then took on that certain look—one that promised a kiss.

"Only over the moon?" She pressed a finger into the dimple in her cheek. "I think my response should garner more than the same reaction a hunter gets over receiving his favorite setter!"

Louis closed the gap between them, and pulled her into his arms, the warmth a comfort and thrill. "I'd be far beyond the universe—in the heavenly realms—if you'll be my wife."

He covered her mouth with his, the heat spiraling down to the toes of her boots. As he deepened the kiss, he drew her closer and she trembled.

Darren nudged his snout between them and whined. Children's voices carried from nearby and they broke their embrace.

Sonja giggled. "That's quite the offer…"

A line formed between Louis's dark brows.

"I mean, about being over the universe—considering that you'll have us living at the Poor Farm." Sonja burst into a fit of laughter.

Louis bowed at the waist. "Madam, let us establish that I do have a penchant for slight exaggeration."

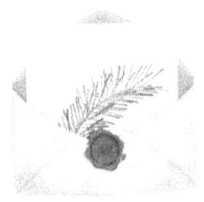

Chapter Nine

Sonja huddled with the pastor's wife at the sanctuary's exit. Christmas was feeling merry after all. She adjusted the ecru lace collar on the new burgundy silk moiré gown from her mother and father. Rows of rosy lace covered the bodice over the full skirt. Beneath, her new white satin petticoats swished every time she made the slightest movement. She couldn't help grinning.

"The pageant couldn't have gone any better, Miss Hoeke." Mrs. Mathews clutched little Joshua's hand.

"Thank you." Sonja squeezed in as close to the beautiful, ebony-haired woman as she could, but both of their festive gowns could have filled the entranceway had they stood there, instead of to the side. Teresa Mathews wore her prettiest gown today, constructed of velvet in a soft violet that perfectly matched her striking eyes. Satin piping edged the wide cuffs and the high collar. The entire bodice was embellished with tiny beads and embroidered roses.

The Mathews other son, little Daniel, raced toward the church vestibule, where candy boxes were being distributed to church members.

"Daniel Mathews! Only take one!" The preacher's wife turned and called out as the three-year-old grasped a box in each hand and turned, grinning.

Mrs. Mathews shook her head. "Boys can be trying."

Other parishioners chatted with each other and greeted Sonja and Teresa as they exited the sanctuary and headed down to the church hall, where a reception awaited.

"I've never seen the church so packed for our children's program." Mrs. Mathew's violet eyes twinkled in merriment.

A twinge of unease traveled up her spine, making Sonja aware of the hundreds of buttons on her dress's back. "Is there something you're not telling me?"

Her friends, Lila, Mamie, Christina, and Letitia, rushed toward Sonja, all dressed in their finest and giggling.

Mrs. Mathews arched a slender, dark eyebrow and laughed.

Her pals grabbed Sonja's arms and pulled her to the choir room.

"This is scandalous," Sonja protested as they locked the door, Mamie pressing her bustle toward it and laughing.

"What is scandalous, my friend, is a young woman living at that farm with a gentleman and no benefit of marriage."

"Indeed." Lila turned and lifted an ethereal lace veil from a square white box.

Christina laughed. "Time to put that on for the wedding."

"What wedding?" Heat flushed Sonja's cheeks and she pressed her hands to them.

Mamie opened a box on a table positioned against the back wall. She pulled out four small floral bouquets.

Then Mamie handed Letitia a larger bouquet. Gorgeous hothouse flowers spilled out of the arrangement, trailed by burgundy ribbons that matched Sonja's gown.

She accepted the flowers and drew them to her nose, inhaling the perfumes of the roses and lilies. "These are beautiful!"

"Pastor Mathews found them in the reception hall when he arrived." The girls glanced between one another.

"The washerwoman your parents hired told him they'd come in by rail this morning and delivered directly to the church."

A chill coursed up Sonja's arms as she examined the perfect blossoms. Her parents hadn't hired anyone to clean the hall—the churchwomen had cleaned and prepared it for the pageant when the janitor fell ill. But if he was sick, why was Mr. Zinker seated out there watching his daughter, who was dressed as one of the sheep?

Louis's stranger had to have managed this somehow. He'd shared over dinner how she'd been in his office. Sonja laughed. Would the mysterious woman be there even now?

"It's like a reunion in here." Mr. Wenham gestured to a nearby couple, his British accent thickening.

A strongly built man and slender woman joined them.

Thomas gestured to each. "This is my sister, Emily, my brother-in-law, William."

Louis extended his hand and shook William's hand. "Pleased to meet you."

Emily nodded and Louis did the same. No handshaking for this lady. He was firmly back in the Midwest now and the Wenhams were English immigrants, brought there by the land grant program as many farmers had been.

"This is Louis Smith Penwell, the young man made good who I'd told you about. The whole community has come out to welcome him back."

"Nice to meet you, son." William's gray eyes met his own as the older man shook Louis's hand. His clipped accent differed from Thomas's, which held more of a note of the English countryside.

"We live in Palo," Emily said shyly, her accent less pronounced than her husband's and brother's. "We farm."

"Nice to meet you, ma'am."

"Lloyd!" Mr. Wenham's brother-in-law turned and ran after a blond-haired boy who rushed toward the cake table, where other boys gawked over the seven-tier creation.

Emily pressed a hand to her chest. She turned to her brother. "Your nephew is a rapscallion—he takes after you!"

The cake rescued, William returned with the squirming boy tucked under his arm.

Louis tweaked the boy's ear gently. "I suspect your only punishment on this festive day shall be to remain seated between your parents until cake is served!"

The family laughed and another group moved toward Louis.

Now, one after another, as Louis waited in the church hall, festooned with swags of holly and ivy and bits of lace, old friends—yes friends who'd remember poor Louis Smith—had come forward and congratulated him on his immediately impending nuptials. He'd be exhausted before the vows were ever said.

Tables were covered with evergreen and berry arrangements, the punch bowl attendants giggling as they pointed at him. Louis's collar suddenly felt too tight.

A silence settled over the large rectangular room as Reverend Mathews was assisted up onto a sturdy chair.

"Attention everyone! The wedding will take place in here because our bride was a little busy in the sanctuary until now." He pointed to Louis. "And apparently the groom may not have informed her about the wedding part of the reception!"

Laughter erupted.

"Although I didn't know Louis when he lived here before, I'm delighted to welcome him to our membership."

People clapped and several men moved forward, all dressed in suit jackets. Mr. Hood, Ronald, Mr. McLaughlin, and Dr. Queen leaned in. "We're your groomsmen, in case you'd not figured that out yet."

Louis shook each man's hand.

Four young women, in pretty church dresses, their hair upswept, jewelry adorning their necks, preceded Sonja into the room. He strained to see her, his heart pounding. Would she be angry with him? Was he presumptuous? Of course he was, but he couldn't help grinning.

Louis fingered the note in his jacket pocket. The third book had been marked by the note. *Make Christmas future the best ever, Louis. Don't give up love when it is right before you. Don't make the mistakes I made. God gave you a second chance at love—I just helped Him out with those plans.* No signature. But he knew it was from the stranger.

He'd given up the nightmares, he'd rested easy, he'd forgiven. And now Louis knew—God had brought him healing via his substitute bride. Thanks be to God—who'd placed Louis in Shepherd to restore him. This was the beginning of the best Christmas ever—and of the first day of his new life—in the one place he'd never have chosen. But who was this woman? He'd be troubled until he knew who had intervened in so many ways on his behalf.

Mr. Hood came alongside Louis, standing between him and Ronald, who was to be his best man. He reached into jacket pocket and pulled out a telegram. "This arrived earlier. I think it is from your grandmother."

"Grandmother?" Both grandmothers were both gone. Louis accepted the message, as the men looked on.

The telegram operator's ruddy cheeks grew redder. "Isn't Nona a name an Italian grandmother uses?"

"Yes, but I'm not Italian. And I have no surviving grandmothers." That he knew of, anyway. And when the county officials contacted his grandparents' last known address, all indications were that they'd passed away. Louis scanned the telegram.

May God restore all you have lost. Until we cross paths again, Non un Angelo.

Louis stifled a chuckle. So the philanthropic stranger wasn't an angel, after all. "It's not Nona, Mr. Hood—it's

Italian for 'Not an Angel.' It's from a rather mysterious friend."

"Too bad—Italian grandmothers are the best," Mr. Hood elbowed Louis good-naturedly.

Ronald pointed to the preacher, who was waving them forward. "I think we best get a move on."

Thank goodness no one could see Sonja's shaking knees beneath the full skirt of her beautiful gown. They were about to marry yet she'd not heard the words she'd been waiting to hear from her sweetheart. Did he feel as she did?

"I love you." Louis took her hand in his and probably would have kissed her had Reverend Mathews not cleared his throat loudly.

"I love you, too." Sonja's whispered reply was lost amid the titters of laughter in the room.

"Dearly beloved…"

She heard Reverend Mathews as he spoke, and she repeated her vows at the proper times, but Sonja wasn't sure she'd remember any of that part of the marriage ceremony. But when Louis was allowed to kiss his bride, that part seared into her soul. His warm lips covered hers, claiming her as his wife. He'd held her for what seemed like an eternity, when Teresa Mathews tugged on Sonja's arm and pointed to the cake.

"Darlin', if you want there to be any left for you two to cut, you'd better shorten this part and take it up later." She winked at Louis, who actually seemed to blush.

A half dozen boys, mostly Wenhams and their cousins, darted out from behind the cake table, all with various amounts of frosting on their faces.

Louis guided Sonja over to the table, the crowd parting, and applauding as they walked. Her cheeks heated and she lowered her gaze to the wood floor ahead of her, strewn not with rose petals or rice, but bits of wedding cake. Would their home be filled with little boys who loved cake?

After they'd cut pieces of cake for one another, Sonja's maid of honor slipped in, along with Ronald, to continue serving.

"I want to show you something that Mr. Hood gave me." Louis handed her a telegram and she scanned it, her Latin coming in handy.

"Not an angel." She laughed. "I did wonder."

"He thought that it had been signed Nona, but as much as I wish I had a grandmother, I do not." Louis drew in a deep breath. "Although I have no surviving kin that I know of, I do now have a mother-in-law and father-in-law, sisters and brothers-in-law, nieces, nephews, three wards— including Ronald here until he turns eighteen—and a huge dog!"

"Might as well count him too, he eats enough." She kissed his cheek.

They watched as Lila and Ronald served cake to her parents. Her father fairly burst at the seams with pride. He held the plate aloft and called to Sonja, "Mother's letting me have cake today!" He cackled as he headed off with her mother, who rolled her eyes.

Her eldest sister and her husband turned from where they stood by the punch bowl, beaming. Sonja thought she'd spied them alighting from a carriage earlier, but Mother had convinced her that it must only be someone who looked like her sister. Had she spied her in the pageant she'd have known something was definitely afoot.

Sonja tapped the name on the telegram before handing it back to her husband. "Although this lady may not be an angel—as her signature indicates—you certainly do have angels looking over you."

"You're right. I do. I have you." Louis pulled Sonja into his arms and kissed her. "My beautiful wife. You're not a substitute bride. But the wife I've chosen. The one God had planned for me all along."

The End

Author's Notes

As I began this story, I wanted a rushed move for a bachelor to an unexpected new position, and a promotion, with his employer—the railroad. And I wanted a Poor Farm near Shepherd, Michigan. History treated me kindly, because both a major railroad center and a Poor House were in the area during the time frame of my story.

Poor Farms, or Poor Houses, have a long history in particular before the Social Services movement began.

Yes, they really were called Poor Houses or Poor Farms, depending upon where you lived. I also refer to the location as the County Farm in this book. Some places housed only adults. Some had a mix of children and adults, as this book portrays. Some separated men from women and some did not. I was surprised to see the residents called inmates, but in some situations, apparently they were treated somewhat like prisoners—as they did in Victorian England as well.

When I worked in Lower Michigan, I visited Shepherd many times. It is easy to get to today, via the interstate. The town boasts a rail museum and I was delighted to visit Shepherd and give a presentation at the library and tour the museum! It's a delightful small town full of lovely people.

I struggled with a couple of my characters' names—in particular one who wasn't alive in the story but was a huge influence upon the hero and heroine. As I searched for Poor Farms in Michigan, I came across the right "friend" for Sonja. In real life, a Cora Degley was buried in a potter's field near Shepherd. The article indicated that (sic), "It is probable that the medical department at the state unversity will demand the body for dissecting purposes." Reading that sentence made me shudder. I used Cora's name and we had her moved to a church cemetery, protecting her from the body snatchers from the university (or "unversity" as indicated in the post!).

Salt River, Michigan, burnt in 1887. The original Salt River was home to a sawmill and flour mill, which used the river's power. Then the railroad came into the town in 1885. Stone buildings were built by Mr. Shepherd near the railroad line.

My novel, *My Heart Belongs on Mackinac Island*, a Maggie Award winner, includes more Welling characters as do many of my other books! See my book list at the end of this novella.

As to the mysterious woman's identity—she is also in a few of my other books and she gets her own HEA and storyline in *Anchored at Mackinac*!

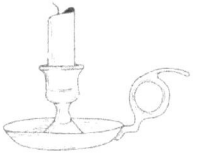

Acknowledgements

Thank you, Father God. I don't know why this wasn't supposed to be the short story I planned but you know! God bless my little family for tolerating my frequent home location being in "story world"!

Thank you to the helpful citizens of Shepherd, Michigan who keep their history alive. Special thanks to Joyce Noyes who was so much help. She and her husband, Larry, are both charter members of the Shepherd Area Historical Society. Her husband is currently the President of the Society and Joyce served as an officer for many years. Joyce is also co-chair of the Little Red School House Museum in Shepherd who shared with me about Salt River, Shepherd, and the maple syrup traditions that they still have today.

Thank you to Patty Smith Hall and Niki Turner, who served as diligent critique partners to me on this project! I appreciate my editor, Narielle Living's hard work and any errors are my own.

Thank you to my beta readers: Sonja Hoeke Nishimoto (and thanks for the use of your name!), Gracie Yost, and Tina Rice. Regina Fujitani my early Beta reader has gone on to be with the Lord, but she really blessed me. I appreciate my advance readers: Caryl Kane, Deanna Stevens, Britney Adams, Sydney Anderson, Ann Ellison who has also gone on to heaven, Kay Davis Moorhouse, Martha Phillips, and Chris Granville.

God bless my Pagels' Pals group, who provide me so much encouragement!

A big hug and thank you to Libbie Cornett, my best friend, who introduced me to Christian historical fiction several decades ago. I am so glad God put us together and I don't believe I'd be writing Christian fiction if you'd not started me on that path!

Author Biography

Carrie Fancett Pagels, Ph.D., "Overcoming With God", is a bestselling, award-winning, Christian fiction author. Working as a psychologist for twenty-seven years failed to "cure" her overactive imagination. Raised in Michigan, she returns most summers.

Website: www.CarrieFancettPagels.com

Social media: Facebook Author page, Pinterest, Instagram, YouTube, X, LinkedIn, and more!

If you enjoyed this novella, a review is very much appreciated!

Carrie Fancett Pagels' Books

Mackinac Island Romances series:
> *In Desperate Straits - Prequel*
> *My Heart Belongs on Mackinac Island*
> *Anchored at Mackinac*
> *Mackinac Island Beacon*

> Associated books:
> *Mercy in a Red Cloak*
> *Dime Novel Suitor*
> *The Sugarplum Ladies*
> *The Substitute Bride*
> *Behind Love's Wall*

Mackinac Cottages series:
> *Butterfly Cottage*
> *Lilac Cottage*
> *Tandem Cottage*

James River Romances series:
> *Return to Shirley Plantation*
> *Shenandoah Hearts*
> *Dogwood Plantation*
> *The Steeplechase*
> *Love's Escape*

Mackinac Straits Lumberjacks Series:
> *The Fruitcake Challenge*
> *The Lumberjacks' Ball*
> *Lilacs for Juliana*

Requilted with Love
Tea Shoppe Folly
Saving the Marquise's Granddaughter

"Snowed In" in *A Cup of Christmas Tea* collection (Guideposts, 2013) Out of print.

www.ingramcontent.com/pod-product-compliance
Lightning Source LLC
Chambersburg PA
CBHW070509130626
46555CB00003B/1223